W9-CIC-785

BRAINWASH

by the same author:

The Hard Hit
Death Of A Big Man
Who Goes Next?
Pool Of Tears
A Nest Of Rats
Do Nothin' Till You Hear From Me
The Jury People
Thief Of Time
A Ripple Of Murders

BRAINWASH

John Wainwright

ST. MARTIN'S PRESS   NEW YORK

Copyright © 1979 by John and Avis Wainwright
All rights reserved. For information write:
St. Martin's Press, Inc.,
175 Fifth Avenue, New York, N.Y. 10010
Manufactured in the United States of America

Many men would take the death-sentence without a whimper to escape the life-sentence which fate carries in her other hand.

T. E. Lawrence
The Mint

CHAPTER ONE

The room. We must start by describing the room because in effect the room was the stage upon which the whole drama was performed. The stage, and more than the stage; it was also the backdrop, the wings and the scenery. And the door was the curtain which, when it opened, allowed one of the star actors to enter on perfect cue and thereafter deliver his lines without prompting and with immaculate timing.

But a room is merely part of a building – a box within that building; and a room gathers within itself some of the atmosphere of the building of which it is a part.

The building was a police station.

It is odd, but understandable, that police stations have an aura peculiar to themselves. Even police officers, to whom police stations are merely places of work, catch a whiff of this aura. It is, one must suppose, the accumulative dregs of past and countless guilts; the scent of lawlessness and the subtle emanation of sin which in some way has soaked into the stone and woodwork of the place. It can produce a feeling of disquiet. A gentle chill of guilt, felt even by the innocent.

No police station is ever a happy place. Lighten it with acres of window-glass, illuminate it with all the brilliance of strip-lighting, give it parquet floors and keep those floors like polished mirrors, but these are only externals. That which is difficult to describe still lurks beneath the gloss. To the law-breaker it is still 'the bogey house' and the colloquialism is very apt.

The room, then, was part of a police station.

It was one of those multi-purpose rooms which give an impression of architectural error; as if the architect, or perhaps the builder, had miscalculated and been left with an area of floor space not specifically earmarked for any determined purpose. It was smaller than the Charge Office, but considerably larger than any of the purpose-built Interview Rooms. Its size approximated the average living room in any street of middle-class semis. To the eye it was a perfect cube; the walls were all of a length, and the height was no more and no less than the length and the breadth. There was one door and one window. The door was solid-looking and well-fitting. The window was high, proportionately narrow and multi-paned; the lower three rows of panes were of frosted glass.

A double radiator beneath the window gave off enough heat to soften the chill, but without providing real or comfortable warmth. There was a wash-basin in one corner of the room, complete with hot and cold taps, a tiny mirror and a chrome-plated rail upon which was draped a folded hand-towel. Twin strip-lighting gave the room its light; a harsh, blue-tinged light, which seemed to eliminate shadows and at the same time drain the room of what colour it might have had. The walls were colour-washed. Silk finish. Stone-coloured, perhaps? Yes, on close examination, stone-coloured. But in the fluorescent glare, and at a distance of more than a yard, a curiously opaque grey. The floor was covered with 'government issue brown' lino, the colour of plain chocolate, hard-wearing and polished to a sheen of dull reflection.

The room was sparsely furnished. Only the bare essentials occupied what seemed to be an over-abundance of floor space. There was a table; polished-topped, scratched and, at one corner, ink-stained, with a drawer at one end. The table was positioned, almost geometrically, beneath the strip-lighting. On the surface of the table was a cheap blue tin ash-tray with the words 'Player's Navy Cut' embossed around its circumference. A tubular steel and canvas chair was situated at each end of the table, and a third similar chair stood by the wall, alongside the door.

This, then, was the room. The stage. The portion of the police station which, for the moment, was reserved for a kill-or-be-killed confrontation between a suspect and his interrogator. An arena where, within the rules of law and British justice, a duel had been arranged.

The door opened and a uniformed constable ushered the suspect into the room. The constable made a brusque waving motion towards the table with one hand. The suspect moved his head in a tiny nod of understanding, then seated himself on one of the tubular steel and canvas chairs.

The constable closed the door, moved the chair which was near the door a few inches farther from the wall, then he, too, sat down.

The suspect murmured, 'May I . . . ?' Then he cleared his throat, and said, 'May I smoke?'

The constable said, 'Why not?'

It was exactly 10.30 p.m.

CHAPTER TWO

In the Charge Office a conference was under way. Four
men were exchanging opinions, expressing points of view
and offering suggestions. They formed a huddled quartet
in one corner of this heart of the police station; beyond
the hearing of the switchboard operator and out of earshot
of the two night-duty clerks who were busying themselves
with the teleprinter flimsies, the day's quota of road accident reports and the records of the scores of minor incidents which had gone to make up the division's working
day, and all of which had to be filed and referenced during
the less hectic hours of the night shift. The foot-patrol
men were out on the streets. The motor-patrol men were
cruising the district in their squad cars. The shift-change
was a mere thirty minutes gone and the night's activity
had not yet wound itself up to a normal, steady pattern.

The quartet was composed of two uniformed officers
and two C.I.D. men : a chief inspector, an inspector and
two sergeants. The chief inspector was the acting divisional officer, the uniformed officer responsible for the
running of the division while the divisional superintendent
slept. The inspector was the senior divisional C.I.D. officer.
One of the sergeants was a detective. The second sergeant
was the office-duty sergeant for the night.

'It's him,' said the detective sergeant.

The detective sergeant was a portly man, prematurely
grey and with the outward appearance of a would-be
dandy; would-be for the very good reason that his salary,
a wife and two sons precluded any serious attempt at
sartorial splendour. Nevertheless, well-dressed, well-shod,

well-shirted and -tied, and with his grey hair parted and brushed back into very becoming wings above each ear. Like many plump men he was surprisingly light on his feet; he held himself well and with an unself-conscious pride in his profession. He was a Lancashire man from Manchester and a faint twang of his county's manner of pronunciation invaded his speech. He was a good detective.

He said, 'You get the feeling, sometimes. And you know you're right.'

'Did you arrest him?' asked the detective inspector mildly.

'No. Just to come along to clear up some points in his statement. That's all.'

'And he raised no objection?'

'No.' The detective sergeant shook his head. 'His wife wanted to come with him, but I talked her out of it. I told her it was just routine. To check a few facts. No more than a few minutes.'

'I see.'

'He accepted that?' The chief inspector sounded suspicious. 'That cock-and-bull story. He accepted it without question?'

'He found the body.' The detective sergeant spread his hands, palms upward and at waist height. 'As far as he's concerned that's all we know. Why shouldn't he accept it?'

'And that *is* all we know,' murmured the detective inspector.

'But,' muttered the office-duty sergeant, 'we suspect a hell of a lot more.'

'Coincidences, perhaps?' suggested the chief inspector.

'Oh, come *on*, sir,' protested the office-duty sergeant. 'Three times? Three separate sets of coincidences? That's like believing in fairies.'

The chief inspector looked worried and annoyed. He was at least ten years younger than the office-duty sergeant and was wise enough to know that the elder man 'carried' him through any awkward spots which might crop up during their shared tour of duty. He was aware of his own comparative inexperience and, like so many other inexperienced officers, he regarded 'the book' as his Bible. Stay with 'the book' and the law, not the man, carried the blame; the law was an ass – statute law, case law and even common law – an ass, compiled by donkeys; it was biased on the side of the law-breakers and the bias could only be cancelled by means of what the old hands laughingly called 'The Ways and Means Act'. In short, by bending the law to suit a specific purpose. By chancing your arm. By forgetting 'the book' and deliberately crawling out on a limb.

In the past he'd seen the office-duty sergeant use 'The Ways and Means Act' on numerous occasions. On drunks, on hooligans, on general riff-raff who had to be controlled. And he'd approved, he'd even smiled to himself at the po-faced solemnity with which the office-duty sergeant had quoted non-existent laws and claimed non-existent powers.

In the past the trick had always worked.

But this time ...

Barker was no drunk. No hooligan. No riff-raff. And moreover the crime was murder and rape. Or, to be chronologically accurate, rape followed by murder. And on three separate occasions in less than six months.

Something far more substantial than 'The Ways and Means Act' was necessary this time. This time 'the book', and only 'the book', could keep everybody out of big trouble.

The chief inspector said, 'You're sure you didn't actually arrest him?'

'I didn't arrest him,' said the detective sergeant.

'He didn't think he was being arrested?'

'No, sir.' The detective sergeant sighed. 'He knew he *wasn't* being arrested. I told him so in as many words.'

'Then why bring him in?'

It was a reasonable question. Reasonable, that is, if you were the acting divisional officer; if you carried the rank which decreed that every baby ended up in your arms, with the possibility of it messing in your particular lap. In such circumstances it was a very reasonable question.

If you were a working jack and held the rank of detective sergeant it was, on the other hand, a ridiculous question. Barker was the bastard responsible. On three separate occasions he'd taken some poor kid, held her down, rammed his chopper into her then, to make sure she couldn't land him behind granite, strangled the poor little bitch. Barker. It had to be Barker. The second two had been carbon copies of the first and to even suggest Barker wasn't the shithouse responsible was pushing coincidence way out beyond the skyline. And all the bull about 'finding' the third victim? That was as old as Eve's gag about 'finding' the apple. They'd already been half-way onto him when he'd 'found' the third victim. That had been the clincher.

Okay strong suspicion, even knowledge, wasn't proof. But what the hell did that mean? That whenever the urge came on he could drag another kid somewhere and rape and strangle *her*? What the hell sort of bobbying was that?

Proof wasn't there: okay proof had to be found. The animal had to be made to break. To sweat bricks till he coughed and provided the proof necessary.

The detective sergeant took a deep breath and said, 'Look, sir, it's him. It's Barker. We're light on evidence, but that doesn't mean we're wrong. If we wait he'll do it again. And keep on doing it. I don't want that to happen. I'm not going to *let* it happen. He's inside because I want somebody to have another go at him. A real go. I want the bugger hounded till he breaks. Till he's *there*.' The detective sergeant held out a hand and closed the fingers into a fist. He ended, 'That's why I brought him in. That's why I'll keep on bringing him in. Eventually, one day, I'll bring him in ... and he won't go out again.'

'I see.' The chief inspector smiled a sad smile. 'A one-man crusade. Is that it?'

'Call it what you like, sir.'

'A defence solicitor might call it harassment.'

'It won't be the first time,' growled the detective sergeant. 'When they get to that, they're almost under. It's the last plea before "guilty".'

There was a moment's silence. An awkward silence, a silence in which the thoughts of what should be played havoc with the thoughts of what was. There was much truth in what the detective sergeant had said. Indeed, allowing for over-enthusiasm, it was all true. Criminals did walk the streets, openly and unashamedly. Wicked men for whom the law was a shield; whose cause was mistakenly espoused by various organisations of do-goodery; whose continued freedom was a perpetual insult to men and women devoted to the task of law-enforcement.

Nor did objectivity come into it.

Police officers were human beings. In the main they were decent, level-headed human beings. That being the case, the rape and strangulation of a child could never be viewed with complete objectivity. Disgust came into it. Contempt also. But, above all else, a fierce, burning determination to nail the culprit and punish him; to stand him in a Crown Court dock, slice his puny defence to shreds and hear the judge pass a sentence which would take one more sub-human out of circulation for as long as possible.

Police officers are human beings and these men were all police officers.

The chief inspector reached a decision.

He said, 'He's in. For whatever reason, he's here. We might as well make the most of it.' He paused, chewed his lower lip for a second, then continued, 'I could, I suppose, get somebody with some real weight down here. The detective superintendent. Probably even the head of C.I.D. That's . . . that's what I *should* do. But if I did . . .' He looked at the detective sergeant. '. . . you'd have your balls chewed off, for a start. Me, too, I shouldn't wonder. To put it bluntly, if we take one wrong step we're both up the creek. Wrongful Arrest, sergeant. And don't tell me you didn't "arrest" him. You've deprived him of his liberty, that and a clever lawyer is all he needs. And I've stood here and let you. Sanctioned it, if only by doing nothing about it.'

The three others waited.

The chief inspector turned to the detective inspector and said, 'Mr Lyle?'

The detective inspector inclined his head slightly.

'Can you pull it off?' asked the chief inspector.

'I can talk to him,' said Lyle.

'Convince him it's not victimisation?'

'Yes.' Lyle smiled. 'I think I can do that.'

'D'you mind? I know I'm asking you to put your neck on the chopping-block along with Bell's and mine. But d'you mind?'

'I'll talk to him,' repeated Lyle.

CHAPTER THREE

The two detectives walked side by side along the corridors of the police station. Suddenly there seemed no hurry. No urgency. Away from the disquietude of the uniformed chief inspector, what they were doing and what they planned to do seemed quite logical. Even necessary and almost mundane. A criminal, a known child rapist and murderer, awaited confrontation.

And that he *was* known, and *was* guilty, was accepted as a simple fact not worthy of either mention or discussion. George Barker was merely lucky. Not innocent. His luck had been stretched to near-breaking-point, but it had held. Suspicion had piled upon suspicion, coincidences had followed coincidences like the endless frames of a paddle-wheel until only certainty remained. But it was a certainty with insufficient proof; a certainty which lacked the necessary evidence required by law.

Put Barker in the dock and for a time you could have made him sweat. You could have convinced a jury that such a string of coincidences – such a weight of circumstantial evidence – merited a conviction: for a time. Until a good advocate rose to his feet to cross-examine. Until the final speech for the defence was made. Until that infernal 'reasonable doubt' was paraded and emphasised and hammered home time and time and time again.

Then would come the acquittal.

And George Barker would walk from the court and, if he so wished, he could button-hole the nearest policeman and explain, in minute detail, exactly how, where and when he had ravished three little girls and, having ravished them, had murdered them as a form of self-defence.

And, he would still have been innocent.

Lyle and Bell knew the law. Indeed they respected the law and worked hard to give the law a practical application. But they also knew the limits of the law. Its weaknesses. Its stupidities. Its utter and, at times, quite lunatic absurdities.

Their job was to circumnavigate these absurdities and, if possible, make the law 'work'.

Therefore as they walked the corridors of the police station they did not discuss the guilt or innocence of George Barker. Their talk centred upon the possibility of ensuring that his guilt was embedded in a foundation of evidence which could not be destroyed.

'He'll be sweating,' observed Bell.

Lyle murmured, 'He's been sweating since his first murder, sergeant. He's no superman. That's our main advantage.'

'Scared.'

'Scared,' agreed Lyle. 'One might almost say terrified. The question is *how* terrified. Terrified enough to break? Or too terrified ever to break?'

Lyle, it must be admitted, did not have the appearance of a policeman. His manner was far too mild. His speech was far too quietly modulated. He had the air of an academician, albeit a cunningly dangerous academician. There was an immediate impression of artlessness. Almost of naïve simplicity. But then gradually the realisation dawned that the quiet courtesy was a scabbard within which was housed a razor blade of accomplished Machiavellianism. Lyle, it was said, could given time have talked the devil from hell itself.

And yet a quick glance did not give that impression. In height he topped the six-foot mark, but only just. His

17

physique suggested a skeleton encased in a body slightly too small for comfort; he was slim rather than thin, angular rather than gaunt. The knuckles of his fingers were a shade on the knobbly side. His cheekbones were prominent and the bone of his jaw could be followed from joint to joint. And his eyes: such eyes are often described in romantic novels, but rarely seen in real life. Genuine forget-me-not blue. They might have held an innocence, had it not been for the ice which seemed to film them when he narrowed his gaze and defied any man or woman to feed him a lie.

His interests gave a clue to the man himself. Chess and bridge were the only two games in which he interested himself and in both he was a player to be reckoned with; team games and outdoor sport of any kind left him un-moved and he was one of the few men in the United Kingdom to whom the F.A. Cup Final, or a test match at Lord's, meant absolutely nothing. His reading was limited to non-fiction: history, travel, biography and a wide span of the various branches of philosophy. In music he preferred the intimacy of the quartet or the quintet rather than the grander sweep of symphony or concerto, his two favourite composers being Haydn and Mozart.

Somewhere in the background, it was rumoured, there was a wife. Or, to be precise, there had been a wife. Her name was unknown and she was never mentioned.

Some four years previously he had come across a cot-tage tucked away in one of the lesser known folds of the dales. A dilapidated, ramshackle tumble of old stones and timbers; once a tied cottage, but now little more than an eyesore in one corner of a field which was part of one of the larger hill farms. He'd bought the cottage and an acre of surrounding land and, for four years, he'd worked and re-built what was to be for him a home and a retreat. The work had been slow, laborious and time-consuming as far as his off-duty periods were concerned. He'd built with his own hands and without either manual or mechanical aid. Stone by stone, beam by beam, he'd created his own phoenix, little less than thirty miles from the police station from which he operated. At first his colleagues had scoffed; no man, however single-handed, could re-build that ruin. And, after he'd proved them liars, they'd insisted that 'commuting' a distance of thirty miles, or thereabouts, was out of the question for a working detective. But again he'd proved them wrong and by this time nobody scoffed, but many were envious. But in fairness it was an envy tinged with admiration.

Lyle, then, could be likened to a perfectly balanced dynamo, quietly and without fuss creating his own limit-less energy from within. A little frightening; a man liked and admired by many, but a man with few friends.

Lyle opened the door of the main C.I.D. Office and walked in followed by Bell. Bell flicked the light switch as he passed.

It was a large room. The eight desks were arranged in two rows of four and, on each desk, the personality of its C.I.D. occupant could be guessed at. Some desks were neat; almost old-maidenish in their carefully laid out array of pens, pencils, rulers and paper-weights. Some had ash-trays, some had not. Some of the ash-trays were nests of goo and spent matches; dottle poked from the bowls of pipes and an overflow of matches from pipe-smokers who had yet to learn the art of keeping the tobacco gently smouldering until it was all ash. Some of the 'in' trays were piled high with work yet to be tackled, others were almost empty. On two of the desks were tiny framed photographs of smiling women – the wives of the detectives who worked from those desks – while on three of the other desks makeshift frames held the glossy nudes cut from the pages of soft porn magazines. Four typewriters were shared between the eight desks; three of them were covered, the fourth was open and still held a half-finished report against its platen.

Along the walls of the room were the filing cabinets. Metal and green-painted, filling all the wall space between the door and windows. An immoderate amount of paperwork, all neatly pigeon-holed and locked away in drawers from prying eyes.

Bell fished keys from his pocket, walked to one of the filing cabinets, unlocked it, pulled open the top drawer and, without hesitation, removed three foolscap-sized manila envelope-files; they were salmon-pink in colour and bore the imprint 'Cathedral Business Wallet'. They were all fat and well-filled with documents and photographs, and across the flap of one was pencilled the name 'Standish', across the flap of the second was pencilled the name 'Wallace' and across the flap of the third was pencilled the name 'Roberts'.

'Standish'. 'Wallace'. 'Roberts'. Very ordinary names. Other than to their parents, very ordinary children; sometimes well-behaved, sometimes aggravatingly naughty; simple and uncomplicated in their beliefs and trusts; occasionally wicked, as all children are, at times unconsciously wicked; occasionally so artless – so supremely *ingénue* – as to bring a lump to the throat and the impossible wish that the adult world might accept a lesson and reach for a similar uncomplicated simplicity.

Three files, three children – all little girls – and three graves. Three occasions when a man had descended to a level below that of the beasts. Three separate accumulations of heartbreak and anger. There . . . neatly tabulated within three separate folders. The 'why?', the 'where?' and the 'how?' . . . but still lacking the 'who?'

Bell dropped the folders onto a nearby desk, closed and locked the filing cabinet, returned the keys to his pocket, picked up the folders and said, 'Okay. How do we do it?'

'We talk.' Lyle had lit a cigarette while Bell had been taking the folders from the filing cabinet. He rolled ash from the cigarette into an ash-tray on one of the desks and continued, 'Specifically, *I* talk. You take notes and act as witness.'

'He's been talked to,' growled Bell.

'I know.'

'By the super. By the chief super. Even by the assistant chief. It's done nothing.'

'You're wrong, sergeant.' Lyle allowed a smile to touch his lips. 'Every interview has softened him up that little more. He's no longer the man who first reported finding Roberts's body. Unless of course he's innocent.'

'The hell he's innocent.'

'In that case he's lived with his guilt since the moment he murdered her. Since the moment he murdered Wallace. Since the moment he murdered Standish. For months in fact. The self-knowledge that he's a child rapist and a child murderer. Plus the knowledge that we suspect him – and more than suspect him. He's a changed man. Whether he's enough of a changed man, remains to be seen.'

'Just talk, then?' There was unconcealed disgust in Bell's question.

'Just talk,' agreed Lyle, gently.

'I can't see what the hell good . . .'

'He's not a criminal, sergeant.' Lyle inhaled cigarette smoke. 'That's his big weakness.'

'Not a criminal! With three kids dead and . . .'

'Not in the accepted sense,' interrupted Lyle. 'He's not our sworn enemy. No previous convictions. Not even a motoring offence. No previous convictions, therefore no previous experience of how we, the police, work. He probably has vague expectations of bright lights and rubber truncheons. Locked doors and third-degree treatment. If he's any sense he knows that's rubbish, that even the American police rarely used such methods and even then only in the distant past, but he doesn't *know*. He hopes he's right – indeed he *is* right – but he's not one-hundred-per-cent sure. That doubt is on our side, sergeant. It's been on our side since the first murder. He's treading strange ground and he's frightened. We don't have to frighten him. The fear's already there. All we have to do is talk. Just talk. He'll break, because his own desire for peace of mind requires him to break.'

'Conscience,' sneered Bell.

'Don't underestimate it, sergeant.'

'A nice little *conversazione*? With a bastard who's strangled three kids?'

'Something like that,' agreed Lyle, mildly. 'With you taking copious notes, of course. In case they're needed.'

Bell chose his words meticulously. He said, 'Inspector Lyle, I did not chance my arm by bringing in Barker for the purpose of organising a quiet little *tête-à-tête* when I could be catching up on lost sleep. Whatever you call them, *I* call them criminals. Scum. Living arguments for the return of the hanging-shed, and if necessary I'd pull the lever. I want him broken, Inspector Lyle. And, if you can't do it, I can.'

'I'll break him,' promised Lyle solemnly.

'I hope so.'

'But with you sitting there recording every word. Every question. Every answer. And without interrupting. I don't want you within his line of vision. I want him to forget you're even there.'

'Okay.' Bell nodded. 'That way for starters. But if it doesn't work . . .'

Lyle ignored the open-ended threat. He said, 'You'll need more than your notebook, sergeant. A clip-board and foolscap, I think.'

Bell opened the drawer of one of the desks, took out a metal clip-board and some foolscap, then left the drawer open.

As they walked from the C.I.D. Office, Bell switched off the lights and closed the door.

CHAPTER FOUR

Having dismissed the uniformed constable from the multi-purpose room Bell settled himself on the vacated tubular-steel and canvas chair by the door. He crossed his legs, positioned the clip-board and foolscap on his knee, took a ballpoint from an inner pocket of his jacket and headed the first sheet of foolscap '10.40 p.m.'

The position of Bell's chair was exactly as Lyle would have wanted it; almost directly behind Barker's back. Lyle and Bell could see each other without hindrance, but their direct line of sight passed within a foot of Barker's left shoulder and Barker was facing Lyle across the length of the table.

As the two detectives had entered the room, Barker had twisted in his chair to view the newcomers. He'd screwed out what was left of his cigarette into the tin ash-tray, then flapped a hand self-consciously to clear the cigarette smoke hanging in the air in front of his face. He'd followed Lyle with his eyes as the detective inspector had walked the length of the table and settled himself in the vacant chair. He'd answered Lyle's silent nod of greeting with a quick, timid smile and now he watched as Lyle chose one of the envelope-files, then placed the two other files carefully on the table top within easy reach of his left hand.

Lyle opened the flap of the chosen file, slipped the contents clear of the manila folder and, without looking up, said, 'My name's Lyle. Detective Inspector Lyle.'

Barker gave a double blink and the blinks seemed to be a deliberate response to Lyle's self-identification.

Still busying himself with the papers, Lyle said, 'We

have a few things we'd like to clarify. A few inconsistencies.' He suddenly raised his head and looked Barker straight in the eyes. 'You've no objections, I hope?'

'No. Er – no.' Barker flushed; as if he'd been unexpectedly caught in some compromising situation. He swallowed, cleared his throat, then said, 'Not at all.'

'It's a little late,' murmured Lyle.

'Th-that's quite all right.'

'Probably inconvenient.'

'No. I – er – I don't . . .'

'But these things happen without regard to convenience, or the fact that they might interfere with the regularity of daily routine.'

'No. It's – it's not inconvenient. I assure you.'

'Nevertheless, it's very good of you, Mr Barker.' Lyle's lips bowed into a smile. 'I can think of many people who might have refused Sergeant Bell's request to come here at this time of night.'

Barker did not answer.

There was, if not fear, apprehension in Barker's expression. But the impression was that apprehension was no stranger to those eyes, to that face. He was a timid mouse of a man, a man crushed into everlasting submission by . . . something. Or somebody. His hair was flecked with grey, as was the carefully trimmed moustache which he wore on his upper lip. In some peculiar way, the moustache seemed to add to the overall impression of insignificance. He wore an obviously off-the-peg blue serge suit, complete with waistcoat, a white shirt and a wine-coloured tie. The cuffs of the jacket were a little frayed, the elbows a little shiny with wear and, around the collar, tiny confetti scatterings of dandruff could be seen.

Lyle sorted his way through the clipped and stapled papers as he said, 'Sergeant Bell tells me your wife would have liked to come with you.'

25

'Er – yes. She – er . . .'

The remark dwindled away into silence.

'I've no objection. No objection at all.' Lyle looked up and continued, 'If you'd like your wife present while we . . .'

'No!' The exclamation quietened into more normal speech. 'No, thank you. It's – er – it's not necessary.'

'The choice is yours, of course.'

'I'd prefer her not to be here,' muttered Barker.

'As you wish.' Lyle folded the stapled papers and read from the one he had isolated from the rest. 'Now. First things first. Your full name's George Barker?'

'Er – yes.'

'Address 43 Caladine Crescent?'

'Yes.'

'Your age is forty-four?'

'Forty-five, actually. It was my birthday last week.'

'I see. Thanks.' Lyle took a pen from his breast pocket and made a small alteration on the quarto-sized sheet. He said, 'You work for the local authority?'

'Yes. I'm a wages clerk in the treasury department.'

'Just so.' Lyle scanned the typewritten sheet for a few moments, then looked up and said, 'Briefly, according to this, you took a dog for a walk. Your next-door neighbour's dog. That was the evening you found the body of the girl, Roberts. Gwendolen Roberts. You returned home, telephoned the police, then made this statement to a Detective Sergeant Allcock in the presence of Detective Superintendent Shaw.' Lyle looked up from the statement form and added, 'Right?'

'Yes, sir.' Barker nodded.

Lyle placed the palm of his hand on the statement form in order to keep the file open at its required place. He no longer consulted the statement as he asked the questions.

'The dog?' he said.

26

Barker said, 'My neighbour's dog. A fox terrier. Rough-haired.'

'You like dogs?'

'Yes, very much.'

'Then why your neighbour's dog? Why not your own dog?'

'I – er – we don't have a dog.'

'Any particular reason?' asked Lyle, mildly.

'What?'

'You say you like dogs. Like them very much. And yet you don't own a dog of your own. Why?'

'My . . .' Barker sighed, then said, 'My wife.'

'She doesn't like dogs. Is that what you're saying?'

'She's a – a cat person.'

'Ah, I see. You have a cat?'

'No.' Barker shook his head.

'She doesn't like dogs, but she likes cats. Presumably you have had a cat.'

'No.'

'Ah . . . *you* don't like cats?' Lyle smiled, understandingly.

'Yes. I like cats,' said Barker.

'Really?' Lyle sounded a little surprised.

Barker said, 'I like all animals. All of them.'

'But you don't own a cat and you don't own a dog?'

'No.'

'Do you own a pet of any sort? Goldfish? Canary? Anything?'

Barker's 'No,' was barely audible.

'Strange,' mused Lyle. 'You both like cats. You – personally – like all animals. I wonder . . .'

He left the question unanswered, raised one shoulder enquiringly and waited.

Barker moistened his lips, then said, 'The truth is my

wife only *says* she likes cats. I – I think . . . No, I *know*, when she was a little girl she had a cat. It – er – it died.'

'All animals die,' observed Lyle, gently.

'Yes, but . . .' Barker looked miserable and embarrassed.

'The shock?' suggested Lyle.

'No. Not that.' Barker took a deep breath, then said, 'The fact is Edwina is very house-proud. As a woman, you see. As a child she loved cats . . . this cat of hers. But now . . . she's very house-proud.'

'Some women are that way inclined,' sympathised Lyle. He spoke as if he had a lifetime's experience behind him.

'They're . . .' Barker stopped, then in little more than a whisper, continued, '. . . sometimes very difficult to live with.'

'Quite,' agreed Lyle.

Lyle raised a hand and took a pair of spectacles from his breast pocket. He slipped a folded, freshly-laundered handkerchief from an inside pocket, shook out the folds, breathed on the glass of the spectacles, then polished the lenses with the handkerchief. It was a pause in the interview. The first pause and, in some odd way, a silent warning. The preliminaries were done with. The obligatory touching of gloves had been performed. The fight was about to begin.

They were half-moon spectacles and when Lyle hooked them over his ears they transformed his face. They made him look more benign, and yet more dangerous. More cunning. More mentally agile.

He closed and straightened and stapled papers before he continued the conversation.

Then, he said, 'Dogs. Fox terriers, in particular. They find things. They nose things out long before the human eye can catch sight of them. Rabbits, for example.'

'Ye-es, I suppose so.' Barker was suddenly on the defensive.

'This dog. What do you call it?'

'Spot.'

'Spot. Did he chase rabbits?'

'Sometimes.'

'Only sometimes?'

'Whenever he . . . Y'know, whenever rabbits were about.'

'On the common, for example?'

'Yes. On the common,' agreed Barker.

'Spot didn't find the body,' observed Lyle, gently.

'No.'

'*You* found the body.'

'Yes.'

'Before Spot.'

'Yes.'

'I find that odd,' said Lyle. 'One of the – er – inconsistencies I mentioned. One of the reasons for Sergeant Bell asking you to come here this evening.'

'The dog?' Barker looked puzzled.

'That the dog, especially a fox terrier, didn't sniff out the body first. Or,' Lyle smiled, 'perhaps he was on a lead.'

'No. He wasn't on a lead.'

'Odd.' Lyle shook his head, slowly. 'Very odd.' Then without giving Barker time to comment he asked, 'You take Spot for a run often, do you?'

'Yes. Very often.'

'How often?'

'Most evenings. I like a walk before I go to bed. I call for Spot and he comes with me.'

'A very regular occurrence?'

'Yes.' Barker nodded.

'And on the evening of the third?' Lyle raised questioning eyebrows above the half-moon spectacles.

'Yes. On that evening, too, I . . .'

'Mrs Beeston says not,' interrupted Lyle softly. He tapped the papers on the table with the tip of a forefinger. 'I can quote, if you wish, Mrs Beeston's statement.'

'Oh!'

'Your next-door neighbour. The owner of Spot.'

'Yes, of course.'

'She states, quite categorically, that you *didn't* call for Spot on the evening of the third. You usually do. She verifies that. But on that particular evening you didn't.'

'Oh!' Barker's eyes flickered right and left, as if seeking some avenue of escape. He muttered, 'D-didn't I?'

'You should know,' observed Lyle.

'Yes, I . . . I should. I could have sworn I did.'

'Indeed,' agreed Lyle. 'Your statement says you did.'

Barker almost groaned, 'Perhaps she's mistaken. Mrs Beeston, I mean. Perhaps she doesn't remember.'

'Mr Falkener – you know Mr Falkener of course?'

'Of course.' Barker nodded.

'Mr and Mrs Chalmbers – you know them?'

'Yes.'

'A youth, a teenager, Thomas Morebank?'

'Y-yes. I know him.'

'They saw you that evening,' said Lyle, in a flat voice. 'They all say the same. They didn't see a dog – didn't notice a dog with you – same thing. They all know Beeston's fox terrier.'

'Everybody . . .' Barker's voice rasped off into silence. He swallowed, rubbed the back of a hand across his lips, then said, 'Everybody in the district knows Spot.'

'The dog wasn't with you.' Lyle made it a statement of fact, not a question.

'He was. I'm sure he was.'

'Mrs Beeston says you didn't call for it.'

'I did. I'm sure I did.'

'Falkener. The Chalmbers. Morebank. They saw you, but they didn't see the dog.'

'They're mistaken. They must be.'

'Mistaken?'

'Spot runs ahead sometimes. Most of the time. You know how dogs race around when they're taken for a walk. Spot did that. He – he was forever sniffing around in bushes. Clumps of grass. Hedgerows.'

'Sniffing around?' Lyle peered over the tops of his half-moon spectacles.

'Yes. Like all dogs do. Especially fox . . .'

'He didn't sniff out the body. Did he?'

'No,' breathed Barker. 'He didn't sniff out the body.'

Lyle returned his attention to the stapled papers in front of him. He riffled through the file until he reached the photographs. Police photographs. Harsh black-and-white photographs, with a hard, glossy finish. Pornographic in the sheer violence of every minute detail. He tore one of the photographs from the file, and pushed it across the table towards Baker.

'Look at it,' he said quietly.

'I – I'd rather not. I don't like . . .'

'*Look at it!*' For the first time Lyle put real authority in his voice.

Barker reached out a hand. Slowly. Reluctantly. He touched the photograph, pulled it nearer, turned it and stared at it with shocked eyes.

'That's how she was,' said Lyle. 'How we found her. How you left her. In the ditch by the wood. That's how her clothes were. Ripped to hell. Remember?'

Barker nodded dumbly. Unable to take his eyes from the horror of the photograph.

'Blood,' said Lyle, softly. 'Blood everywhere. You can't rape a seven-year-old without there being a lot of blood.

On her legs. On what's left of her clothes. Everywhere!
Fresh blood, Barker . . . and the dog didn't find it?'

'He – he didn't,' groaned Barker.

'This dog. Running around. Sniffing all over the place.
And he didn't find *that*?'

'I found her.' The words were like heartbroken sobs. 'I
found her, not Spot. Don't ask me why. How. Why he
didn't find her. Just that . . .'

'Just that the dog wasn't there. That's why he didn't
find her.'

Barker raised his eyes, stared across at Lyle and said,
'On oath. Anything. Spot was with me, but he didn't find
her.'

'That's your story?'

'It's the truth.'

'What you've said all along?'

'What else can I say?'

Lyle leaned forward fractionally, then in a very reasonable – very reasoning – voice said, 'Barker. Sit in my
chair. This chair. Listen to what I've been listening to.
Know what I know. Know what all these statements say.
Beeston, Falkener, Chalmbers. Morebank. They've nothing to gain. No reason why they shouldn't tell the truth.
Then what you're saying. Would *you* believe it?'

Barker seemed unable to answer. His lips moved, but
no sound came from his mouth.

'Would *you* believe it?' repeated Lyle.

There was a remorselessness about the question. An im-
placability which refused to be ignored. The question was
going to be asked and asked and asked again. Forever.
Into the dim unknown mists of eternity, that question was
going to be asked . . . until it received an answer.

For a third time Lyle said, 'Would *you* believe it?'

Barker shook his head. Jerkily, as if his neck muscles
had seized and refused to function properly. He continued

to shake his head as he spoke. Again, as if unable to stop the jerking, left-right-left movement of his head, once it had started.

He groaned, 'No. No, I wouldn't believe it. I don't expect you to believe it. I don't expect anybody to believe it. Ever.'

CHAPTER FIVE

So bloody easy, thought Bell. *Little more than ten minutes and the bastard's crumbling already. He's been proved a liar. He's admitted he's telling lies. That his statement's a pack of lies. That even he wouldn't believe all the crap he's been feeding to us.*

Superintendents. Chief superintendents. They've all had a go at him and nothing. Then Lyle cracks him as easily as cracking an egg.

On such a little thing. A bloody fox terrier. A nothing. Those statements. Falkener, Chalmbers, Morebank. Not one of them says the dog wasn't there. Just that they didn't notice the dog. A something. A nothing. But Lyle fastened onto it. Good lad, Lyle. Dig into him. Crucify the bastard. You've got him ... keep at him.

Not too promising, thought Lyle. *Justification for Bell's half-cock stupidity, perhaps. Too scared to make a formal complaint. Not a hope in hell of bringing a charge of Wrongful Arrest. But beyond that, what?*

A fox terrier. Ah, well ... you can't put a fox terrier into a witness box, more's the pity. And if you could what the hell would that prove? There are some damn silly dogs around. Even fox terriers. Some of them couldn't smell fresh meat if it was dangled within an inch of their nose. The dog didn't find the body. Big deal! That damn dog was everybody's friend, if the statements are to be believed. Everybody's friend, anybody's friend. The original canine clown. So much for the why-didn't-the-dog-sniff-out-the-corpse line of questioning.

And yet there's guilt somewhere. Somewhere under all that snivelling fear there's something else. Guilt. Guilt of some sort.

Lyle, old cock, you'd better change tactics. Play him a little. Give him some rope . . . could be he'll wrap it around his own neck.

CHAPTER SIX

Bell jotted '11 p.m.' at the head of a fresh sheet of lined foolscap.

Lyle reached across the table and slid the photograph away from Barker's gaze. He picked it up, glanced at it, murmured, 'Not nice,' then replaced it in the file before him. He removed the half-moon spectacles and placed them on top of the file. Then he took a packet of cigarettes from his pocket, opened it, shook the cigarettes loose and held the packet towards Barker.

Barker hesitated, then took one of the proffered cigarettes.

Lyle snapped a lighter into flame, leaned forward, lit Barker's cigarette then his own.

They smoked in silence for a few moments, then Lyle said, 'You knew her, of course.'

'Who?'

A sliver of Barker's returned composure snapped off as he asked the question.

'The Roberts kid. Gwendolen. Gwen, I think that's the name she usually answered to.'

'Yes, Gwen.' A great sadness stirred in the depths of Barker's eyes. 'I knew her. Most people knew her. She was a lovely child. A very happy child.'

'Trusting,' mused Lyle. 'She must have been very trusting.'

'Nobody would have harmed her,' said Barker, softly. 'Nobody who knew her.'

Lyle said, 'Somebody did.'

'Yes.'

It was a simple, flat affirmative. It carried no emotion. The sorrow from the eyes did not ride the tone. And yet, the sadness stayed in the depths of Barker's eyes.

'You have no children?' said Lyle.

'No.'

'From choice?' Lyle drew on the cigarette, then added, 'It's none of my business, of course. It bears no relationship whatever to your being here, but . . .'

'From choice,' interrupted Barker.

'I see.'

'My wife has always been . . . afraid.'

'Understandable,' murmured Lyle.

'I'm sorry, inspector. I don't agree.'

For the first time something approaching anger tinged Barker's words. This little man, this outwardly insignificant human being, allowed the glimpse of an inward fury to show.

He said, 'A woman gets married. Sex may not be all-important. It may not be the main ingredient of marriage. But it is a part. Sex, and motherhood – if motherhood is possible. A woman who marries, while not believing at least *that*, perpetuates a confidence trick. She takes, but refuses to give.'

'Your marriage?' asked Lyle, gently.

'Of course.'

'I'm sorry.' Lyle's sympathy sounded genuine.

This time Barker drew on his cigarette before asking, 'Are you married, inspector?'

'Er . . .' Lyle hesitated, then said, 'No.'

'Then how the devil do you know what I'm talking about? By what yardstick? By what impudence do you claim the right to appreciate what I mean?'

Lyle did not reply.

Something was happening inside Barker. Something which was tearing at his very guts, something which had been tearing at his guts for years. The sadness had left his eyes. The flatness had left his voice. He seemed in some strange way to grow; as if the bitterness within him had exploded and was filling him out and making him taller. He was no longer the meek, apologetic Barker of a few moments ago. Instead he was, momentarily, a complete man. A complete male animal, with a hurt which called for great and terrible revenge.

For the first time he looked, and sounded, as if he was capable of murder.

He said, 'Twenty-five years, Inspector Lyle. That's a long time. A time for celebration. For silver wedding anniversaries. That's how long. Twenty-five years of near-celibacy. Sex being a dirty word. Sex being something bestial. To be told that you're filthy. Depraved. A pervert.' He took a long, deep draw on the cigarette and his fingers trembled with controlled rage. He almost snarled, 'The douche. The condom . . . never forget the condom. Not the pill. To use the pill would be tantamount to an admission that she copulated. To tell a doctor – an outsider – that she and her husband actually coupled. So, no pill. Always the condom. Then, as if I'd injected her with some foul disease, the douche. God only knows what patent medicine muck she washed herself out with, but she . . . she . . . she . . .'

The rage left him with a rush. He seemed to deflate, to return to his previous meekly submissive personality. The transformation was utter and instantaneous; like the slamming of a door, or the turning off of a tap. The sadness returned to his eyes, his shoulders drooped and he gulped in breath, like a man at the end of a killing race, then exhaled it in a long, shuddering sigh.

'She killed your unborn child.'

Lyle ended the sentence for him. Gently and with understanding.

Barker moved his head in a single, heartbroken sob and, for the first time, there was complete rapport between interviewer and interviewee.

CHAPTER SEVEN

This rapport. This coming together of minds.

Lyle, old hand at the interview game that he was, knew that he had passed a minor watershed; that an interview is not a glorified quiz; that a mere question-and-answer session is a stagnant exercise with very little hope of progress.

A true interview, a real interrogation, is a locking together of two opposing personalities. There is give and take on both sides. There is, if not mutual admiration or mutual respect, at least mutual recognition. The Q.C. skilled in the art of cross-examination performs a verbal ballet sequence with the witness, in which both parties are equally important. The same with an experienced police officer. He knows that a successful interview is not too far removed from a duet. A duet with equal parts. With point and counterpoint, melody and descant, harmonies and cross-harmonies. Sometimes the interviewer is on the ascendant. Sometimes the interviewee.

Lyle knew this.

Bell did not.

To Bell an interview was a manoeuvre based upon harassment. 'To make the bastard cough.' To bully, to intimidate, to frighten.

But when the interviewee knows that to 'cough' carries with it the almost certain conviction for triple rape, followed by triple murder, what fear can overcome *that* fear?

Bell, like scores of other police officers, could have named men and women known to have committed major crimes. *Known*, by the police, to have committed them, but never brought to justice. Bell would have said, and believed, that these unpunished law-breakers had never been interviewed 'hard enough'. But Bell would have been wrong. All of them had been questioned, sometimes for hours on end, but none of them had been *interviewed*.

The difference then. Lyle knew he had to give something of himself to Barker, before Barker in turn parted with some small portion of *his* personality. Like buyer and seller, there had to be a recognised contract; an offer, an acceptance and a consideration. A deal, in fact. Part of Lyle for part of Barker. Part of Barker for part of Lyle. But the crunch would come when Barker wanted one more part of Lyle but, in return, could only offer his own guilt.

That was the deal. That was the rapport.

And Lyle knew that the interview, proper, could now get under way.

CHAPTER EIGHT

They lit fresh cigarettes. Again from Lyle's packet.

Lyle leaned back in his chair and said, 'The shock of finding her. There in the ditch. It must have been very great.'

'It was.'

'Did you recognise her?'

'I . . .' Barker hesitated, made a vague movement of his shoulders, then said, 'Yes. I think I did. Not facially, of course. She was lying face downwards. By her clothes, I think. By the gym-slip and the blouse. They were her regular clothes. School uniform.'

'But you recognised her?'

'Yes.'

'What about Spot?' asked Lyle. 'Was he with you at the time? When you found her, I mean.'

'No. He was running around in circles. You know how dogs behave, when they're enjoying themselves. I remember I called for him, and . . .' Barker stopped in mid-sentence. He frowned, stared at the surface of the table for a moment, then looked up and said, 'That's *it*.'

Lyle raised questioning eyebrows.

Barker said, 'Mrs Beeston's right. Of course she is. That evening I *didn't* call for Spot. He was already out. Playing in the crescent. I just called and he came. He knew. I usually take him with me on my walk and he was there. He just came along. I didn't have to call next door to pick him up.'

Lyle smiled and nodded.

They smoked in silence for a few moments.

Then in a very conversational voice, Lyle said, 'Mr Barker. You're not a fool. You know why you're here.'

'Because I'm . . . under suspicion. Or I take it I am.'

There was no outrage in the answer. No anger. No surprise.

Lyle said, 'There are rules to this game. This game of Murder Enquiry. Necessary rules. Otherwise we start every enquiry in a vacuum and that won't get us far. The next-of-kin of the victim. The man or woman who reports finding the body. From the "off", they head the list of suspects.'

'Yes. I . . . understand that. Naturally.'

'After them comes everybody who knew the victim. Not necessarily hated the victim. Just knew him . . . or her. You'd be surprised how many people have been murdered by so-called "friends".'

'I see.'

'We start with quite a list,' explained Lyle. 'And from that list we eliminate.'

'And I have yet to be eliminated,' murmured Barker.

'You have yet to be eliminated,' agreed Lyle.

'And that,' said Barker, in weary tone, 'not counting the other two child-killings. I'm still a "probable" . . . right?'

'Unfortunately.'

'Because I happened to be at Southport. And I happened to be at Bridlington.'

'And now you "happen" to be here.'

'At home.'

'Again.' Lyle's voice had slowed until it was almost a drawl. He moved the half-smoked cigarette in vague and airy gestures as he talked. They might have been two friends having a friendly discussion in the comfort of their club. Neither man tried to dominate the other. Lyle said, 'Again put yourself in our shoes. Southport. The dunes

43

to the south. The body of a child is found. Pauline Standish. An eight-year-old child. Raped. Then murdered. Strangled. Your car was seen parked in Birkdale. Within a mile of those dunes. A mistake – a minor mistake, perhaps, but a mistake – it was parked where parking was prohibited. The car was empty. The number was taken. It was eventually traced to you. Unfortunately – I say unfortunately because, had the circumstances been otherwise, your innocence or guilt might have been more firmly established – Standish's body was not found until three hours after the police had taken the number of your car. It was a routine, minor traffic infringement. Remained so for two days. Until the police at Southport had completed their "eliminations". Then you were visited and questioned by Detective Sergeant Bell.'

Barker said, 'I gave a full explanation.'

'You gave *an* explanation,' corrected Lyle with a smile. 'A quiet drink. Alone. From what you've just said a small taste of unaccustomed freedom. Just the one drink. Then you returned to Southport. To your sister's home.'

'She was ill,' said Barker. 'It was my reason for being at Southport. My sister, Edith, had been seriously ill. She'd had an operation. I visited her for three days, until she was well enough to return home. My wife . . . My wife and Edith aren't friends. That's why I went alone. Then, as you say, a slight taste of freedom. Freedom from my home environment. One glass of beer, that's all. But I happened to park my car in a wrong place.'

'And at a wrong time,' added Lyle.

'It would seem so,' agreed Barker.

'And Bridlington?' asked Lyle, interestedly.

'You know the facts, inspector. I made another statement.'

'Remind me, please.' It was a gentle request, made in a pleasant voice.

44

Barker suppressed a sigh, then said, 'There was a N.A.L.G.O. conference. An annual thing. This year, it was held at Bridlington. I have been elected as the local N.A.L.G.O. representative. I attended. These conferences are dreary things. Necessary, I suppose, but dreary. The evenings tend to become a little riotous. Boisterous might be a better word. A little noisy, a little too much drinking for my taste. I took a walk along the sea-front as far as Flamborough. I enjoyed the walk. I returned to the hotel and went straight to bed. And that's all.'

'Not *quite* all.' Lyle enjoyed a lungful of cigarette smoke before he continued. 'Seven-year-old Rosemary Wallace can't be dismissed so readily. One more child-rape. One more child-murder. Another "Pauline Standish". Her body was found in Dane's Dyke next morning. It had been there all night.'

'I didn't go near Dane's Dyke,' protested Barker. 'I don't even know where Dane's Dyke is.'

'Within strolling distance of Flamborough. Indeed nearer to Bridlington than Flamborough . . . supposing you didn't go all the way to Flamborough.'

'But I *did* go to Flamborough.'

'Ah, yes.' Lyle smiled benignly. 'When I say "you", I mean whoever murdered Rosemary Wallace. Assuming the murderer came from, and returned to, Bridlington.'

'You mean *me*!' The flare-up of impatience coloured Barker's face.

Very gently Lyle said, 'I take it that is not meant to be a confession?'

'For heaven's sake!'

'Bear with me, Mr Barker.' Lyle stretched out a hand and squashed his cigarette into the ash-tray. He met agitation with composure. He drawled, 'The topic was – still is – police procedure when investigating murder. The business of "elimination". The North Yorkshire police

45

"eliminated". Next-of-kin. The person who found the body. Everybody who knew the dead child. It was a good enquiry. Within fourteen days they'd widened the net until it scooped up all the meetings, conferences, get-togethers taking place at that particular time. Including the N.A.L.G.O. conference. They sent requests for all people known to be visiting Bridlington at that time to be seen. To be questioned.'

'By assistant chief constables? By detective superintendents?' The two questions held bitterness, splashed with contempt.

'In your case,' agreed Lyle, smoothly. 'And – correct me if I'm wrong – by a detective chief superintendent. You seemed to have a – er – genius for being around when little girls were raped and murdered. First Southport. Then Bridlington. Now, ten days ago, Gwendolen Roberts. That one required the chief superintendent. And a very long session. You were lucky not to be arrested.'

'I know.'

Barker's contempt had evaporated, but the bitterness remained as he acknowledged the truth of Lyle's observation.

'The police,' said Lyle with a wry smile, 'must of necessity have suspicious minds.'

'You think I killed her.' It was a statement, not a question.

Lyle straightened in his chair, leaned forward, rested his forearms on the surface of the table and linked the fingers of his hands.

He looked directly into Barker's face and, very deliberately, said, 'Yes. We think you killed her. Which in turn means we think you raped, then strangled, all three. Carbon-copies, Barker. Whoever did one did them all. It's why you're here, Barker. I don't have to tell you. I've already said. You're not a fool. You know *exactly* why.

46

But, to cater for fools, the law requires me to spell it out to you.'

There was a silence. One of those silences which seem to vibrate with the very absence of sound; which have no beginning and no end and are therefore timeless. A silence as piercing, and as positive, as any scream. The two men faced each other across the length of the table in that use-it-for-anything room. Face to face. Eye to eye.

Barker moved first.

He placed the spread-fingered palms of his hands on the table, in a first movement towards rising to his feet.

In a steady voice, he said, 'I came voluntarily, inspector. I was asked and I came. Now I'm going. We both know where we ...'

'Sit down, please.' Lyle's tone was neither commanding nor officious, but it caused Barker to relax his arm muscles and sink back onto the chair. Lyle continued, 'One more thing the law requires me to do. George Barker, you are now under arrest on suspicion of murder. That being the case, you are not obliged to say anything unless you wish to do so, but whatever you say will be taken down in writing and may be given in evidence.'

CHAPTER NINE

It was so damn stupid. So damn, *damn* stupid. You had a name – a killer, a child-killer – there, on the slab. Five minutes, ten minutes at the most, and in a very matter-of-fact voice he was going to tell all. He was aching to spill his guts. A man like Barker. Puny. Unimportant. One more little turd in the whole dung-heap of human rottenness, and he was on the point of purifying his miserable little soul.

He was no villain. No 'Mr Big'. No perverted head of some 'firm', hawking terror and filth within its own carefully marked 'territory'. He was a creep. A creep who measured his manhood against schoolchildren.

And inside, bet on it, his guts were churning and tying themselves into ten thousand knots. Inside his kinky little skull he was screaming to confess. Aching to share a guilt sky-high and too tall for him to carry alone.

He was *there.*

He hadn't even needed pushing. One little puff, less than it might take to extinguish a candle, and he'd have toppled.

The 'frighteners'? Who the hell needed the 'frighteners' to drag the truth from a nobody? Barker's own conscience provided its own 'frighteners'. Always the same. The easy ones. The pushovers. They were there to be egged on; they'd been 'seen' by superintendents, chief superintendents, Christ knows who else and they were ready to spill. To *anybody.* To the rawest recruit. To the dumbest copper in the whole damn force.

They were *there*!

Then the fornicating Judge Rules upped and smacked you in the teeth. The rigmarole of the Official Caution. 'You are not obliged to say anything.' So stop being a mug and keep your mouth shut.

Hell only knew how crimes ever got themselves detected.

Lyle had left his chair. He stood, hands deep in the pockets of his trousers, feet planted firmly apart, and stared at the non-reflective panes of frosted glass in the window. He had his back to Barker as if to hide the expression of disgust which mirrored his thoughts.

Without turning, as if talking to himself, he said, 'You're allowed a telephone call. One telephone call.'

Barker didn't answer.

Lyle said, 'A solicitor. You have the right to telephone your solicitor. If you don't have a solicitor we can give you a list. We can't suggest which one, they're all listed. If you can't make up your mind we'll even give you a pin. Make your choice that way. It's as good a way as any.'

Barker still didn't answer.

'Your wife, perhaps.' Lyle continued to speak with his back to the table, facing the frosted glass of the windows. 'She'll wonder where you are. She might be worried. Ring her. Tell her. Tell her what's happened.' He paused, pressed his lips together, widened his nostrils and took a deep breath, then said, 'One telephone call, Barker. Sergeant Bell will take you to the Charge Office and let you make it. It's on the house.'

Barker remained silent.

'Okay.' Lyle shrugged, without moving any other part of his body. 'Turn out your pockets. The lot. Everything on the table. Sergeant, check that they're empty.'

Bell said, 'Yes, sir.'

From behind his back Lyle heard the scrape of the chair as Barker stood up. The tiny noises of articles being

49

placed on the table top. The occasional mutter of Bell's short-tempered remark.

Lyle divorced himself from the other occupants of the room. He removed his jacket, hung it on the peg behind the door and rolled up his shirt sleeves. He unstrapped his wrist-watch and slipped it into a pocket of his trousers. Then he walked to the corner wash-basin, ran hot water and, like a surgeon preparing for an operation, he soaped his hands and wrists with the cheap yellow soap, rinsed them, then dried them on the hand-towel.

Then he re-strapped the watch to his wrist, rolled down his sleeves and buttoned them at the wrist, but left his jacket behind the door.

It was a gesture. Symbolic. Something so many working detectives do, many times throughout the day. A 'washing of hands'. As if to keep the filth within which they worked from contaminating their skin. Or, perhaps, like Pilate removing a responsibility for subsequent injustices; indicating, via this symbolic cleansing, that the law is their master and not their slave.

Slowly, it seemed with some reluctance, Lyle returned to the table.

Bell looked at him questioningly.

'Everything on the table, sergeant?'

'He's clean, sir.'

'Good. Go back to taking notes, sergeant.'

'Yes, sir.'

Lyle turned to Barker and, like a father sadly reprimanding a grown-up son, said, 'Sit down, Mr Barker.'

Barker sat down. Bell returned to his chair by the door and took up his clip-board and ballpoint again.

Lyle stood at the table and for a few moments touched some of the various items on its surface. Ordinary run-of-the-mill items; the sort of junk to be found in any man's possession. The cheap plastic wallet. The cheque-book holder. The inexpensive gaudy ballpoint pen. The opened packet of cigarettes. The throw-away lighter. The key-wallet, holding three keys. The handkerchief, the comb and the tiny collection of coins. Such ordinary things. Such everyday things. And their owner had just been accused of, and arrested for, just about the foulest crime in the book.

Just like that. Like it happened so many times. Indeed like it happened more often than not. No hair-raising car chase. No wild, cornered-rat fight. No spitting and snarling and four-letter words. Just two men talking; one of the men reaches a decision and, as of that moment, the other man is in serious peril of his liberty, virtually his liberty for the rest of his life.

Policing.

Lyle picked up the wallet, returned to his chair, opened the wallet and fingered his way through the contents. A driving licence. A certificate of insurance. A receipt for the repair of a lawn-mower. A couple of library tickets in Barker's name. And some photographs.

Lyle examined the photographs.

He stared at one showing a stern-faced woman wearing severe, no-nonsense tweeds; a two-piece, neatly cut and tailored and obviously cared for.

Lyle turned the photograph to face Barker and said, 'Your wife?'

'Yes.'

'She'll have to know,' said Lyle, gently. Almost sadly.

Barker said, 'I don't want to see her. Tell her. You'll have to tell her . . . I realise that. But I don't want to see her.'

'She might want to see *you*.'

'I doubt it.' The bitterness made Barker's expression and voice ugly.

'She's your wife, Mr Barker. For better, for worse. Remember? She's the woman you married.'

'Inspector.' Barker closed his eyes for a moment, then ran the palm of a hand across his hair. He said, 'What you've just done she did days ago. Weeks ago.'

'Y'mean ...'

'She accused me.'

'Oh!'

'She accused me. She tried me. She found me guilty. Whatever you do – whatever the law eventually says – that's her verdict and she won't alter it. She "knows".'

'Knows?'

'Everything, inspector. One might say she invented E.S.P.'

'Fortunately,' Lyle smiled, 'second sight is not yet admissible as evidence in a court of law.' He lowered the photograph, pushed the wallet and its contents along the table, then slid one of the unopened manila envelope-files nearer. It was the file marked 'Standish'. As he opened the flap and took out the contents, he said, 'Let's start with the Southport job, shall we?'

CHAPTER TEN

'Standish,' mused Lyle. 'Pauline Standish. Speak no ill of the dead – in particular, of the violently slaughtered – but the fact remains she was not a well-loved child.'

'I wouldn't know,' said Barker.

'Of course not. But for your information: a drunken father, a slut of a mother and she herself, despite her years, was known to the police. A "teeny-rocker" . . . that's the label they give themselves. Punk rock. Whatever that means. She was old for her years. A known tease . . . and probably more than a tease.'

'I wouldn't know,' repeated Barker.

'Perhaps,' said Lyle, mildly, 'I'm making excuses for you.'

'I don't need an excuse, inspector.'

'You might. The day might arrive. Let's say I'm filling in some of the gaps you may need in your defence.' Lyle ran a finger up and down the edge of the inch-thick pile of paperwork relating to the case. Slowly. Meditatively. As if concentrating upon his choice of information. He murmured, 'Eight years old. The press chose their photographs with care. From the family snapshot album. They even touched 'em up a bit. To take that glint from her eye. Some of it. But she still looked what she was. An eight-year-old tart.'

'Why tell me this?' asked Barker.

Animation, of a sort, had returned to his voice. The shock of the arrest, and the breathtaking certainty implicit in the words of the Official Caution, were wearing off. It was a technique. Lyle was using it well. Gradually – very gradually – the vital rapport was being rebuilt.

53

Lyle said, 'You're in a privileged position, Mr Barker. Like us. Like the police. The general public are not party to such secrets. It wouldn't be right. The disillusionment might be too much. An eight-year-old? Innocence, but of course. Teddy bears, dolls . . . naturally. Pencils, crayons, Walt Disney movies, candy-floss. The expression, "an eight-year-old" . . . that's the impression it evokes.'

'But – er – she wasn't?' Barker's curiosity was aroused.

'Pauline Standish?'

'Was she . . . y'know?'

'She was a little bitch,' said Lyle, bluntly.

'How?'

Lyle's finger stopped its up-and-down journey along the edge of the file. He flicked his way through the papers, until he found the one he was seeking. He checked his facts.

Then he said, 'From Mrs Standish. Her mother . . . and mothers don't usually put their name to a list of faults of their murdered daughter. But true. All checked and verified by enquiries. She ran away from home four times. Four times in less than two years. Thumbed lifts. Some of the long-distance boys aren't too choosy. Nottingham. Chester. Norwich. Last time to London. There's some suspicion – rather more than a suspicion – that she wheedled her way into the skin-flick outfits.'

'Skin-flick?' Barker looked puzzled.

'Blue films. Hard porn . . . really hard porn. It goes on. There's a market. Private studios in London. A few in the provinces. Not the usual bash-bash stuff. The so-called "open-legged" shots. Kids and animals, that brand of perversion.'

'My God! You mean they force children . . . ?'

'They don't "force" anybody,' said Lyle wearily. 'That's the mistake people make. Decent people. That a kid of that age has to be *forced*. The bastards who set

54

these films up know life. They know they just have to look around. A kid can be a whore before she reaches her teens. The Persil-washed minds of the British public won't accept that. Can't accept it. The do-gooders shy away from the very idea. But it's a fact. A percentage. Not many, but a percentage. Enough for the skin-flick trade. Damn it . . .' For a second Lyle seemed to allow disgust to surface. 'I've seen 'em. These films. The kids are *enjoying* themselves. The adults? To them it's a day's work. But the kids . . .'

Lyle closed the file and made as if to rise from his chair.

'A cigarette?' asked Barker.

Lyle nodded.

Barker pushed the opened packet of cigarettes an inch or two across the table. Lyle helped himself. Barker took one, then flicked the throw-away lighter with one hand while, with the other, he too took a cigarette from the packet.

When they were smoking, Barker said, 'And this Pauline Standish? You seriously think I'd take a little trollop like that into the Birkdale sandhills?'

'She doesn't carry a placard.' He smiled, then corrected himself. 'She *didn't* carry a placard.'

'Nevertheless . . .'

'I know.' Lyle moved the hand holding the cigarette in a tiny wave. 'The chances are, *she* took *you*.'

'Not that either,' said Barker, gently.

'I know. You were enjoying a quiet pint at the time.'

'Actually half-a-pint. I'm no drinker.'

'But you can't remember which boozer.'

'I didn't notice. Why should I?'

'It might have helped.' Once more, Lyle corrected himself. 'It *would* have helped . . . a little.'

'Do you?' Barker raised the cigarette to his lips.

55

'What?'

'You go into a strange town. You feel like a drink. You go into a public house. Do *you* always notice the name?'

'Do you often do that?' countered Lyle.

'What?'

'Visit strange towns? Patronise strange pubs?'

'I've told you. I'm no drinker.'

'It doesn't often happen, then?'

'Very rarely.'

'Odd.' Lyle pulled a wry, but not unfriendly, face. 'A light drinker. A man who rarely goes into strange public houses. The natural thing – to notice the name of the pub, wouldn't you agree?'

'I didn't,' insisted Barker.

'And such an uncommonly slow drinker,' persisted Lyle. 'A half-pint. That's what you say. And it takes you almost two hours.'

'That's what *you* say,' fenced Barker.

Lyle smiled, and said, 'No. That's what the Southport police say. Your car was parked, where it shouldn't have been parked, for more than ninety minutes. They have it logged. Before the body of Standish was found. As a basis for a road traffic offence. That's slow drinking, Mr Barker.'

'But that isn't against the law, is it?'

'Slow drinking?'

'Or is it?'

'No, that's not yet illegal.' Lyle's smile expanded into a grin. 'Just, shall we say, one more oddity.'

Barker nodded slowly and returned the grin with a slow smile. As if the two of them were sharing a very private joke.

'You can't remember the name of the pub,' sighed Lyle.

'Sorry.'

'Or even its general location.'

'I've been asked that, too. I'm sorry.'

'Just that you parked your car.'

'That's all,' agreed Barker.

Lyle examined the tip of his cigarette and murmured, 'You walked one hell of a way, old son.'

'I – er – I don't follow.'

'Well, now. *We* know where you parked your car. At least the Southport police know. Exactly. Three hundred yards to the nearest pub . . . assuming you used that pub. Farther if you used any other pub. Quite a walk.'

'I like walking. I was out walking when I found Gwen's body . . . remember?'

'I have a good memory, Mr Barker,' parried Lyle. 'But "walking" and "going for a drink" aren't quite the same thing. Add to which one more factor. Just about every pub in Birkdale has a car park. The three nearest to where you parked your car all had. Very good car parks.'

'Perhaps they were full.'

'Thursday evening.' Lyle raised his eyes from the cigarette tip and stared the length of the table. He met Barker's eyes and continued, 'Early Thursday evening. Not the best night of the week for pub trade. Out of season, very much out of season. Every publican in Birkdale has been seen. Every waiter. Every waitress. Every barman. Every barmaid. They all say the same. Locals. No holiday-makers. A bare handful of strangers. Not a busy night so they remember every non-local who took a drink. They'd certainly remember somebody who ordered a half-pint, then took longer than an hour to drink it. They've all been shown your photograph, Mr Barker. Them. Every local they could name. Everybody who might have seen you. In every pub in Birkdale. You're a non-starter, Mr Barker. That one's been well buried, under six feet of good earth. Don't try to dig it up again, please.'

Barker's tone was expressionless as he said, 'I parked my car. I walked to a public house. I had a drink. A half-pint. Then I returned to my car. That's what *I* say, inspector.'

'And *I*,' said Lyle, 'say you're a damn liar. That I don't mind too much, but you're also taking me for an idiot in expecting me to believe it. And that, I *do* mind.'

CHAPTER ELEVEN

The weaknesses. The hairline faults which had to be sought for; faults in a story which on the face of it was far more probable, therefore far more believable, than the truth.

Like a climber working his way up a sheer face. Feeling with his fingers for tiny, near-invisible crevices and handholds. Fighting gravity, with little more than cunning and expertise : that's what it was like.

And lose that slender affinity, that rapport, and you fall. All the way. And there you are back at the foot of the face. Bruised, winded and, for the moment, beaten.

That's what it was like. That was why so very few men could really *interview*. Ask a load of questions? – sure. Lean and put the fear of Christ into the man? – easy. Smack 'em around a little? – illegal, of course, but it had been known.

Lyle could interview. He could climb that rock face, inch at a time, as if he had all eternity at his disposal. He knew all the tricks. Talk, but also listen. Listen, but don't just listen to the words. Speak softly, little interviewer, that way the other guy *has* to listen. Make him concentrate; cram as much of his concentration as possible into what *you're* saying, that way he has less concentration to spare for what *he's* saying.

Thus, plus a few thousand other God-given wiles, the basic technique of interviewing.

But at various points throughout the interview – throughout that crawl up the rock face – a leap was necessary. An accusation; a dive for a handhold which (maybe) wasn't there.

The accusations were part of the interview.

The leaps were part of the climb.

But if you missed . . .

Bell cleared his throat, and said, 'Sir.'

'Yes?' Lyle glanced at the detective sergeant with a half-frown of annoyance wrinkling his forehead.

'Foolscap, sir. I need some more.'

'Fine.' The cloud cleared from Lyle's face. 'Take your time, sergeant.'

'Yes, sir.'

The detective sergeant stood up from his chair, leaned the clip-board against the back of the chair and left the room.

It was a diversion.

Maybe Bell *did* need more foolscap. Maybe he didn't; maybe he was well-versed in the intricacies of interviewing and knew that some slight distraction was called for.

Whatever . . .

Lyle had made the first leap of direct accusation and Bell's interruption had attracted Barker's attention just enough.

Lyle could feel the first wetness of perspiration make his shirt cling to the small of his back. He didn't give a damn. He was still on that rock face . . . and still climbing.

CHAPTER TWELVE

'Off the record,' said Lyle with a smile.

'Is it ever?' asked Barker.

'Until Bell comes back,' promised Lyle.

'I think,' said Barker, slowly, 'you're an honourable man.'

'In this job, it's not easy, but I try.' He picked up the photograph of Barker's wife, cocked a quizzical eyebrow at it for a moment, then said, 'Edwina?'

'She tries to be a good wife,' said Barker, and there was irony in the remark.

'They all do,' said Lyle.

'I often wonder how many succeed?'

'Not too many, at a guess.'

'She's a good housekeeper. But that's not the same thing.'

'I know. Some couldn't keep a pig-pen clean.'

'But, y'know, good *wives*.'

'Depends what you're looking for,' observed Lyle.

'A partner,' said Barker simply.

'A partner.' It was almost an echo. The same words, but dim and as from a long way off. Lyle pursed his lips, looked uneasy, then seemed to reach a decision. He said, 'Earlier. I lied to you, Barker.'

'Oh!'

'When we were talking about Mrs Barker. Getting married. Children. Remember?'

Barker nodded.

'I said I wasn't married.'

'And you are?'

'On paper.'

'I'm – er – I'm sorry. You must know what it's like . . .'

'No. Not like you. Not the way *you* mean.' Lyle's eyes had a faraway look in them, as he continued, 'Too much the other way. That was my problem.'

'Was?'

'She blew. "Split" . . . that's the expression she used. She "split".'

'With another man?' Barker's probing was gentle and without malice.

'At a guess. Who knows?'

'You never made it your business?'

'To find out? No.'

'Why not?'

'She's a human being. I married her. I didn't buy her . . . I didn't own her.'

'You – er – you loved her presumably.'

'A presumption.' Lyle's eyes returned to the here-and-now. His voice hardened a little. 'A rebuttable presumption. I must have loved her, or thought I did.'

'And now?'

'How,' asked Lyle drily, 'do you feel about your wife? About Edwina?'

'I'm a weak man.' Barker made the admission without shame or hesitation. 'A so-called "white-collar worker". In the main we're a breed apart. For advancement you always agree with the man above you. Kick against the system – use a blue ballpoint, when *he* prefers a black ballpoint – you're finished. You stay in the same grade. You start an office boy. You end an office boy.'

'You've advanced a little.'

'By saying "Yes".'

'Oh!'

'Little dictators, inspector. That's what we are in local government. Those of us who carry any authority. The decent men, the decent women, they're all on the lower rungs, that or they become sick to the stomach and leave.'

'And you?'

'I'm unpopular.' Again there was neither shame nor hesitation. 'Those under me dislike me. They dislike me intensely. One might say they almost hate me, perhaps some of them do. I make no mistakes, because I can't afford to make a mistake. Nobody would point out the mistake. Nobody would even think of covering up for me. I make no mistakes, therefore I tolerate no mistakes. Which in turn re-kindles their dislike. Where I am at this moment – whatever happens to me – I can think of nobody who might feel pity. Even sympathy. If I go to prison, they'll be glad. If I don't go to prison, they'll be disappointed and wish I had gone to prison. Guilt or innocence doesn't enter into it. There's a man ready to step into my shoes. Another man ready to step into *his* shoes. That's a good enough reason. That's how much I'm disliked, and how much I deserve to be disliked.'

'It happens.' Lyle raised a hand and massaged the cramp which was creeping into the nape of his neck. He stood up and walked to where his jacket hung, and said, 'A man gets hell kicked out of him at home. He retaliates. He kicks hell out of his subordinates at work.' He took cigarettes and a lighter from the jacket pocket and walked back to the table. 'You're not unique, Mr Barker. It's touch and go whether you're even in a minority.'

Lyle held out the packet then flicked the lighter. When both cigarettes were smouldering he returned to his chair.

He said, 'That hasn't answered my question about Edwina.'

'No?' Barker looked genuinely surprised. 'I thought it had.'

'Analogies.'

'They can sometimes explain a truth.'

'I prefer cat-sat-on-the-mat language. I'm a very simple man.'

'No, you're not *that*.' Barker smiled, inhaled cigarette smoke, then went on, 'Edwina. The seaside postcard situation, inspector. The massive, overpowering wife and the tiny, hen-pecked husband, but in real life it isn't a joke. Consider – the picture postcard situation – would *that* man ever have married *that* woman? A monster for a wife? A mouse marrying an elephant? No. In the beginning they're equals. Both young . . . youngish. Both with visions of a future. A future together. There is love. Or, if not love, something they both mistake for love. Then, gradually, the monster grows. And as the monster grows the mouse shrinks. The bawdy joke – the seaside postcard – takes the situation and masks it in humour. But in fact it is not funny. It is the most unfunny situation a man and a woman can ever get into.' Barker took a deep pull on his cigarette, then said, 'I tell you, inspector. Were I capable of murder, she's the one I'd kill.'

Lyle rubbed the nape of his neck again, then murmured, 'We're all capable, old son.'

'What?'

'Murder. Given external pressures . . . the one crime we can all commit.'

The door opened and Bell entered, carrying more foolscap in his hand.

'Back on the record?' smiled Barker.

Lyle nodded.

Bell closed the door, settled himself on his chair, slipped the new sheets onto the clip-board, and wrote '11.43 p.m.' at the head of the top sheet.

CHAPTER THIRTEEN

And what, thought Bell, *does* that *mean? 'Back on the record?' The cunning old sod. Pumping him. Giving him the old cushy-cushy treatment. The between-ourselves-and-nobody-else-will-ever-get-to-know routine. As old as Adam, but it still works. Especially with a creep like Barker.*

Some old lag – some hard-necked bastard who's heard it all before – and even Lyle would be wasting good breath. But this one. Oh boy! Candy from a kid . . . and the louse won't even know what hit him.

And now, thought Lyle, *he's said it. The word 'murder'. With certain qualifications, perhaps. 'Were I capable of murder.' But the forbidden word has been said. Even that he* might *commit murder . . . that, by implication. Not kids. Not little girls having first raped them. His wife? . . . okay, his wife. But the difference is only one of motive. Hatred or fear. The victim is just as dead.*

Barker, old friend, the sea has not yet turned choppy and, although you don't yet know it, there's a force-ten howler waiting to be thrown right in your teeth when the moment arrives.

CHAPTER FOURTEEN

'Let's turn to Bridlington.' Lyle kept the cigarette in his mouth as he pulled the third envelope-file towards him and removed its contents. He took the cigarette from his mouth, fingered the papers from the envelope-file and continued, 'Rosemary Wallace. A year younger than the Standish girl. A nice kid by all accounts. A good home. Well brought up. An older sister and brother. And, about two months after the Standish killing, she's found in Dane's Dyke. Dead. Sexually assaulted . . . that's the polite term for it. Nothing polite about the crime, though. Nothing nice.' He looked up at Barker and said, 'Well?'

'I was in Bridlington. You already know . . .'

'So were a lot of other people. Residents and visitors.'

'I've already explained to . . .'

'I know what you've "explained", Mr Barker. It's all here in black and white above your signature. We call 'em "statements".'

'In that case . . .'

'One thing you haven't explained. How come you "happened" to be in the Birkdale area of Southport when the Standish kid was killed *and* in the Dane's Dyke district of Bridlington when the Wallace kid was killed. That's an explanation we're all waiting to hear.'

'I can't help you,' muttered Barker.

'It might be difficult,' agreed Lyle, 'but nothing's impossible.'

'You . . .' Barker shook his head in near-defeat. He moistened his lips, then said, 'You think I killed her.'

'Which one?'

'For God's sake!'

66

'Standish? Wallace? Roberts? Which one?'

'The same man killed them all according to you.'

'Well, didn't he?'

'You're conducting the enquiry, inspector. Not me.'

'Barker, don't get smart with me. Don't push what little luck you may think you have left. You're in it, man. Right up to the ears. Be warned. Don't get stroppy.'

And having said it – having delivered the broadside – Lyle knew he'd made a bad mistake.

Barker actually smiled. It was a resigned smile; a smile of complete non-resistance. It carried utter submission and absolute passiveness.

Then, Barker said, 'I'm so used to it, Inspector Lyle. The threats. The bullying. It's part of my life. It doesn't make me angry. It doesn't frighten me anymore. I doubt if it even reaches me . . . not as you understand things. It reaches my ears, perhaps. But not my brain.' He tapped the surface of the table with a forefinger. Twice, gently. Then he ended, 'Be outraged with this table, inspector. You'll get far more response.'

From his chair by the door Bell snarled, 'Hey, louse . . .'

'Shut up!'

Lyle's almost shouted words had the crack of a whip-lash. They carried anger. Real anger, not the simulated anger of a police interrogator. Self-anger. Self-disgust. Oh yes, anger at the man who had quietly defied him; anger at Barker, too. But that was a peculiar anger. An anger which was, in part, spiced with admiration. The anger of a frustrated heavyweight champion who has smashed and bounced his fists at a punch-bag and now knows he'll never split the hide.

And anger which brought a twisted grin of temporary defeat to Lyle's lips.

Barker breathed, 'I'm sorry, inspector,' and the impression was that the apology was quite genuine.

And yet the rapport held and was, in some way, strengthened.

As he stood up from the chair Lyle said, 'You're something of a zombie, Mr Barker.'

'Perhaps.'

As he walked to the door of the room Lyle said, 'Nothing affects you.'

'Very few things.'

As he shrugged his arms through the sleeves of his jacket Lyle said, 'Not tough.'

'That least of all.'

'Just impervious.'

'I've been conditioned, inspector. I have no real feelings left.'

Lyle returned to the chair, re-seated himself, then said, 'Okay. Let's talk to a man with no feelings. Let's go back a little and talk about Bridlington.'

'I was there for a N.A.L.G.O. conference.'

'Check. That I believe.'

'That's all.'

'Not quite "all". A seven-year-old kid makes it rather more than "that's all".'

'I went for a walk.'

'And a child dies.'

'I am not a gregarious person, inspector. The evening drinking sessions irritate me. Annoy me. I prefer solitude.'

'Check. That, too, I believe . . . especially when you're committing child-rape.'

It was a little like throwing beans at a battleship. The accusation was accepted without even a blink. It was returned by a smile which bordered upon pity; as if Barker quite genuinely felt sorry for the man sitting across the table from him.

'Okay,' said Lyle wearily, 'let's talk about this walk you took. From Bridlington to where?'

'Flamborough.'

'Too vague.'

'I'm sorry. I don't see how . . .'

'Flamborough. It covers a golf course. It covers a light-house. It covers a stretch of cliffs. It covers a village and two outlying areas . . . North Landing and South Landing. It also covers a Viking fortification rampart . . . Dane's Dyke.'

'The lighthouse,' said Barker. 'I walked as far as the lighthouse, then walked back to Bridlington.'

'Main road? Cliff top?'

'Along the sands as far as Sewerby. Then along the top of the cliffs.'

'Past South Landing?'

'Probably. I don't know South Landing.'

'Through the village?'

'No, not through the village.'

'But past Dane's Dyke?'

'I keep telling you . . .'

'Mr Barker, it's impossible to get to Flamborough Head – which is where the lighthouse is – without crossing Dane's Dyke. From *any* direction.'

'I'll accept that if you say so. I don't know the district well enough to argue.'

'That at some time in that – er – "walk" you were in Dane's Dyke?'

'Yes. If you say so.'

'Where, next morning, the body of Rosemary Wallace was found?'

'Certainly. If you say so.'

'I try to play this game fairly,' said Lyle, softly. 'What you've just said . . . it's one hell of an admission to make.'

'That I walked from Bridlington to Flamborough lighthouse?'

'That you were in Dane's Dyke the evening Rosemary Wallace was murdered. Dusk, I take it?'

'Ye-es. It was almost dark when I reach the lighthouse.'

'The time's right,' said Lyle, flatly.

'That,' said Barker, with a smile, 'should give you some satisfaction.'

'But *you* didn't kill her?'

'No, I didn't kill her, inspector.'

'Was the lighthouse flashing?' asked Lyle.

'Oh, yes. It was flashing before I reached the headland.'

'And the weather?'

'A sea mist. Sea frets, I think the locals call them. Fairly thick.'

'How thick?'

'Fifty-yard visibility . . . thereabouts. Not much more.'

'And when you reached the lighthouse?'

'I stood there. At the headland. Looking out to sea. Just – y'know – thinking. Or, perhaps, not thinking. Relaxing.'

'Just you?'

'Yes, just me.'

'Watching the sea mist?'

'Yes.'

'Watching the lighthouse beam?'

'Yes.'

'Peace, eh? Just you and the sea and the mist. And what else?'

'Nothing.'

'Sea birds? Gulls?'

'It was dark, inspector. Gulls don't fly much in the darkness.'

'Surf?'

'Oh, yes. I could hear the surf hitting the rocks and cliffs around the point. It was very soothing.'

'But nothing else?'

70

'No. Nothing else.'

'No people?'

'No.'

'No voices?'

'Not that I can remember.'

'Nothing?'

'Nothing. It really was very soothing . . . for a man like me.'

'Okay. You stood there. For how long?'

'Ten minutes. A quarter of an hour, perhaps. Certainly no more than twenty minutes.'

'And then what?'

'I walked back.'

'To Bridlington?'

'Yes.'

'Which way?'

'The same way I'd come. Er – no – not quite, I didn't go down to the beach at Sewerby. I walked along the path.'

'Back to your hotel?'

'Yes.'

'And to bed?'

'To my room. I read a little. Then I went to bed.'

'That,' said Lyle politely, 'is a very nice fairy story. But – forgive me – you're a damn liar.'

Before Barker could respond there was a tap on the door of the room.

Lyle's frown of annoyance preluded his impatient, 'Come in.'

The uniformed constable who had sat guard upon Barker, prior to the interview, entered and said, 'Excuse me, sir. Mrs Barker's here. She demands to see her husband. She won't take "No" for an answer.'

Lyle glanced at Barker and saw the near-panic flicker in Barker's eyes.

71

'You want to see her?' asked Lyle, gruffly.

'No! Under no circumstances do I want her to . . .'

'Fair enough, old son.' Lyle waved a soothing hand. He stood up from the chair and spoke to the uniformed constable. 'I'll have a word with her. You sit guard here till we come back.'

'Yes, sir.'

'Sergeant Bell.' Lyle jerked his head.

Bell nodded and gathered up his notes.

As the constable took Bell's place on the chair by the door, Lyle said, 'The caution's been administered, constable. Keep your mouth shut and your ears open.'

CHAPTER FIFTEEN

Lyle peered over the tops of his half-moon spectacles at the irate woman who seemed to dominate the Charge Office.

'Are you in charge, here?' she snapped.

Instead of answering the question directly, Lyle turned to the office-duty sergeant and said, 'The chief inspector?'

'He's out on the streets, sir.'

Lyle turned to Barker's wife, bobbed his head, then murmured, 'Yes, madam. It seems I'm in charge.'

'In that case, I demand . . .'

'No, madam.' The slow, scholarly-looking smile robbed the interruption of much of its sting. 'You may request. You may offer suggestions. You may even object. But, presumably, you are here because your husband is in custody. The charge is serious. You are not his solicitor. You may, therefore, *not* "demand".'

'Are you being . . . ?'

'Impertinent?' Lyle ended the question for her. He said, 'No, madam. Neither impertinent nor obstructive. Merely adamant.'

'I wish to see my husband,' she blazed.

'Unfortunately – unfortunately for you, that is – he has expressed a strong desire not to see you.'

'That's ridiculous.'

'Probably, but quite within his rights.'

'Is he under arrest?'

'Oh, yes.' Lyle nodded, solemnly.

'On what charge?'

'It is,' said Lyle, 'debatable whether I'm legally obliged

to tell you. It is, however, hardly likely that you don't know.'

'He's a murderer.' She breathed deeply through angry and enlarged nostrils.

'No,' said Lyle, mildly.

'In that case why ... ?'

'Whether or not he's a murderer is something a Crown Court will decide. At the moment he's innocent. But as far as the police are concerned suspected of being a murderer. That is the charge he will face ... eventually.'

'Technicalities. Stupid, silly technicalities.'

Lyle thought he detected a slight catch in her voice; a sign of toppling in her outraged anger.

He stood to one side of the still-open door of the Charge Office and said, 'I think we should discuss the matter, Mrs Barker. In the privacy of an Interview Room, perhaps?'

She nodded, stiffly, then walked towards the door.

Behind her the office-duty sergeant raised his eyes towards the ceiling in a silent prayer of thanks.

Bell made as if to follow Barker's wife, but Lyle said, 'Tea, sergeant. I think Mrs Barker would appreciate a cup. I know I would. And some biscuits, there'll be an opened packet in the canteen somewhere.'

Bell looked disappointed. He watched Lyle and the woman leave the Charge Office, then placed the clipboard on a corner of the wall-desk whose territory was that of the office-duty sergeant.

He grumbled, 'A bloody waiter, now,' then walked to where a door led to the stairs and the tiny canteen.

CHAPTER SIXTEEN

Interview Rooms. Again part of a police station; a room, within a police station, and a room built for a specific purpose. A room, it would seem, designed to give a deliberate, claustrophobic effect. A womb, if you will, or, if not a womb, a confessional. Probably a combination of a womb *and* a confessional; a place where one might feel safe and a place where one might divest oneself of evil.

Purpose-built, as an aid to the detection of crime.

The inevitable table; smaller than the table in the multi-purpose room wherein Barker waited. The usual chairs; this time only two and wooden, slat-seated, uncomfortable affairs. Colour-washed walls, colour-washed ceiling, parquet floor and strip lighting. And the multi-paned window – each pane of pebbled-glass – with the standard radiator positioned beneath it.

A room, in other words, without character. A room which promised neither comfort nor discomfort. Which promised nothing. A zero . . . to be filled in, coloured, added to, changed in any of a thousand different ways by the people, and the talk, it temporarily enveloped.

Lyle held a chair for Barker's wife then, when she was seated, he took the second chair.

There was a silence. Awkward in that each wanted to say something, but neither knew how to begin. Then, as so often happens, they both spoke at once.

She said, 'I think I have cause for complaint . . .'

He said, 'Mrs Barker, there are certain things . . .'

They both stopped talking. Lyle made a tiny gesture with his hand and said, 'After you, please.'

She favoured Lyle with a quick, tight smile, then said, 'I think I should have been notified.'

'Of your husband's arrest?'

'Yes. I think you owe me that courtesy.'

'Indeed,' agreed Lyle, politely. 'You *would* have been notified. Within – say – the next hour, or so.'

'It's . . . ,' she glanced at her wrist-watch, '. . . after midnight, superintendent . . .'

'No.' Lyle smiled. 'Not superintendent. Inspector. Detective inspector. Lyle.'

'I don't think that matters,' she said, brusquely. 'The point I'm making is . . .'

'That we should have let you know.' Lyle nodded sombre agreement. Then, he said, 'You have, of course, cause for complaint.'

'I'm glad you think so.'

'But we, too, have a valid explanation, if not a legitimate excuse.'

'Really?'

'Your husband is under strong suspicion. To put it less than that would be less than the truth. But it was necessary to interview him at some length.'

'At some reasonable hour, surely?'

'We don't work office hours, Mrs Barker.'

'Probably not. But, if you've no consideration for him, you might at least have some consideration for me. We go to bed comparatively early. We were on the point of going to bed when your man called and asked George to come here. For "a few minutes", that's what he said. That was two hours ago. Two hours in which I've been left alone to worry.'

'To – er – *worry*?' The question was heavy with innuendo.

'He's my husband.'

'A few moments ago you called him a murderer.'

76

'I don't see the relevance . . .'

'If he's a murderer – as you obviously think he is – you surely didn't expect him back immediately?'

'I expected to be notified.'

'You would have been. You *should* have been,' conceded Lyle. 'I accept the responsibility, Mrs Barker. Please forgive me.'

It was a beautifully modulated apology. It embraced apparent sincerity, plus a near-unique olde-worlde charm.

She compressed her lips a little, then nodded. Satisfied.

Edwina Barker. The photograph from Barker's wallet did her less than justice. The chances were she was one of those non-photogenic people; men and women of whom cameras consistenly lie.

In the first place she was some inches shorter than Lyle had visualised her to be. Not tiny. Not petite. But compact and with a body which, despite her middle years and the less than flattering effect of her clothes, was obviously excellently proportioned. Properly gowned she would have been almost beautiful. She wore very little make-up; a faint dusting of face powder, the lightest touch of lipstick, but nothing more. Nor did she need more. Her face fairly glowed with that combination of good health and regular washing. Her hair, too; straight and severely cut, the style would once upon a time have been called 'bobbed', it had the dull sheen of regular shampooing and a daily brushing. Her eyes were brown: the brown of good and well-cared-for leather, and the lashes were fractionally longer than might have been expected.

The impression was that she rarely smiled; that she rarely allowed herself the luxury of a smile. But with that impression came the certainty that a smile would transform her whole face, make her at least *look* a delightful person.

Lyle took cigarettes and lighter from his pocket, and said, 'If you've no objection, Mrs Barker.'

'Not at all.' Then to Lyle's surprise she added, 'I'll have one, too, if I may.'

The minor ritual of lighting the cigarettes and inhaling that first lungful of smoke seemed to relax some of the stiffness between them.

Then Lyle started gently. Probingly.

He said, 'I've talked with your husband, Mrs Barker.'

'Yes?' She waited.

'Of many things,' continued Lyle. 'Of the murders, obviously. But of other things, too.'

'He won't have told you much.'

'No,' lied Lyle, smoothly.

'He's a very secretive man.'

'Secretive. Or shy. I can't decide which.'

'Secretive,' she insisted.

Lyle rolled the cigarette gently between his fingers as he said, 'Mrs Barker. Before we go any further I feel it incumbent upon me to explain that you can't be called as a witness in the event of your husband being brought to trial. Even if you wanted to, the law won't allow you to be a witness against your husband.'

'Which means,' she said, 'you want to ask me some questions.'

'Please,' Lyle nodded.

'You may ask them,' she said. 'Those I wish to answer, I'll answer.'

'You called him a murderer,' said Lyle quietly.

'I did.'

'Why?'

'He's here, isn't he? In police custody.'

'Ah, but the general impression was – still is – that you have other reasons for making the accusation.'

'Intuition.' She drew on the cigarette, then added, 'Something the police treat very lightly, I don't doubt.'

Lyle smiled and said, 'Something the police themselves often use as a base-line.'

'Really?'

'We call them "hunches".'

'Hunches.' She seemed to savour the word. To try it for taste and, having tried it, found it acceptable. She said, 'Yes, hunches. I have a hunch about George.'

'That he's a murderer?'

'Yes.' She used a very stone-faced tone of voice.

'That he's a child-murderer?'

'Yes.'

'And a child-rapist?'

'Yes.' The tone remained the same, but a look of disgust flitted across her face.

'Three times,' pressed Lyle.

'Yes,' she breathed. Then in a firmer voice, 'Yes, inspector. All those things, three times over . . . and other things.'

Lyle timed the pause then, very gently, said, 'Other things?'

She smoked in silence while she contemplated her manner of answer. Which words to use. How to communicate her feelings to this slim policeman, who looked so little like a policeman. How much she dare tell or, indeed, whether she dare tell all. Then when she spoke it was in carefully modulated sentences. Short sentences. As if delivering the truth to him, bit at a time, giving him the opportunity to digest each fragment before feeding him the next.

She said, 'George is a voyeur. He takes a walk each evening. At dusk. He uses the next-door neighbour's dog as an excuse. He claims to be a bird-watcher. An amateur ornithologist. That's what he'll tell you. That he's interested in bird-watching. He does, indeed, know slightly more than most about bird behaviour. The more common species. It gives him an excuse for carrying binoculars. For tip-toeing around coppices and woods. For walking along the common. For seeking out-of-the-way places where couples copulate. But that's why he goes to such places. Not to watch the bird-life. To watch the sex act. He's a peeping Tom, inspector. He has been for years. To you, perhaps, that makes him a pathetic creature. I've heard that argument. I don't subscribe to it. To me it is disgusting. Degrading. Foul.'

Lyle said, 'You talk as if you know. As if it's more than suspicion.'

'I know,' she said. 'Twice I've followed him. Watched him. Witnessed his perversion. Three times I've caught him – unexpectedly – using his binoculars at the bedroom window. Watching windows of neighbouring houses. Once, about two years ago, he came home with a bloody nose and face bruises. His story was that he'd tripped and hit his face against a log. I didn't believe him. I still don't believe that story. In my opinion he was caught by some young man and given a thrashing. A well-deserved thrashing.'

'Nevertheless,' said Lyle slowly, 'and accepting the truth of what you say. Voyeurism to murder. It's a big step.'

'Voyeurism, to the rape of seven-year-old girls. That, as I see it, is the step. Not a very big step, really. After the rape murder must, of necessity, follow. In order to preserve his so-called "respectability".'

CHAPTER SEVENTEEN

The uniformed constable looked up expectantly as the door of the multi-purpose room opened.

As he entered the room, Bell said, 'The electric kettle's on. Tea's in the pot. Lyle and this bastard's wife want liquid refreshment. Come back when the tea's brewed.'

The uniformed constable remained seated. He looked uncertain and a little frightened.

Bell held the door open and repeated, 'Come back, when the tea's brewed. Well brewed.'

The uniformed constable hesitated, then stood up, glanced at Barker and nodded. He left the room and Bell closed the door.

Bell strolled towards Barker. Unhurriedly. Threateningly. Like a big cat approaching a tethered prey. And as he strolled he talked. Softly. Almost in a whisper. Hate-filled words with which he seemed to be deliberately stoking the fires of his own fury.

'Barker . . . eh? The smooth bastard who can't be talked into a cough. The bloody animal whose weight stops short at kids. The sod who thinks he's going to get away with it.' He reached Barker's chair, shot out a hand, twisted his fingers into Barker's hair and jerked the frightened man's head back. From a distance of less than six inches Bell growled his anger into Barker's face. 'Just you and me now, bastard. Just the two of us. And you're going to spill your lousy guts. Get it? You're going to *talk*. Sing. Go through the whole operetta. Word perfect . . . or God help you !'

Barker was terrified. The terror drained his face of

colour, brought perspiration to his forehead and upper lip, and deprived him of speech.

'Stand up,' said Bell.

Barker straightened himself from the chair. When he was almost upright Bell hit him. The balled fist carried every ounce of Bell's weight and muscle and bedded itself into Barker's body, just below the pit of the stomach, just above the groin. It seemed to go in wrist-deep.

For a split second Barker remained upright. Mouth and eyes wide in a silent scream of anguish. Then he folded his arms across the lower part of his body and crumpled, sending the chair toppling towards the wall of the room. He lay there, curled into a ball, quietly sobbing his pain.

'Who did you kill?' asked Bell, tonelessly.

Barker didn't answer. It was doubtful whether he even heard the question; all his concentration was centred upon the agony inside his guts.

'Who did you kill?' repeated Bell.

Again Barker didn't reply.

Bell stared down at him, without pity, without any real expression, then stepped sideways and around the man on the floor. Barker was on his side, rocking slightly and moaning as he cradled his middle. Bell positioned himself carefully.

'Gwendolen Roberts?' As he asked the question Bell lashed out with his right foot. The toe of his shoe thudded into the vertebrae in the small of Barker's back.

Barker arched his back for a moment, clutched at the point on his spine where Bell's shoe had landed, gave a quick, animal-like, choked-off scream of pain, then curled forward once more and hugged the lower half of his body.

Bell allowed himself a sneering smile of contempt then, as he lashed his shoe home once more, said, 'Pauline Standish?'

Barker huddled himself into a tighter ball; buried his

head in his chest and brought his knees even higher into his body. Despite the teeth gripping his lower lip, a groan of agony escaped and blood trickled from his mouth, as he bit even deeper into his own flesh.

'Rosemary Wallace?'

A third time Bell's shoe toe found its mark on Barker's exposed spine. Again Barker clamped his teeth onto his lower lip, but failed to completely smother the groan of agony.

Bell stepped back and looked down at his victim. There was no pity, no remorse, in his expression. Not a hint of sympathy in his eyes. What there was was naked contempt, mixed with near-fanatical determination.

He righted the fallen chair and replaced it at the table.

Then for a full minute he once more stared down at the injured Barker.

At last he said, 'Get up, filth.'

Barker remained curled on the floor, rocking gently and holding himself.

'*Get up!*' The shouted order was tinged with hysteria. 'Get up. Get back in this chair, you bastard. I'll have the truth out of you yet.'

Barker crawled to the chair. Slowly, painfully, he hauled himself into a semi-crouched position then, using the tubular-steel supports of the chair as a form of leverage, he rolled his punished body into a slumped, sitting position on the chair's canvas seat.

He looked up at Bell. There was fear in his eyes, but something more than fear, too. Limitless derision and something akin to pride.

In a hoarse voice, he said, 'I killed nobody, Sergeant Bell. I can't fight you. I can't stop you from doing whatever you want to do, but I killed nobody.'

CHAPTER EIGHTEEN

'His "so-called" respectability?'

Lyle took the woman's last few words, repeated them and turned them into a probe.

Odd. He was beginning to like this woman; this person who, according to Barker's implied description, was something of a female ogre. Lyle didn't think so. On a snap judgement, he'd say she was a fighter. The antithesis of all 'Women's Lib' had ever stood for, but possessing something the militant 'libbers' lacked and, for obvious reasons, never included in their arguments. The natural dignity of her own sex. She was a woman; the contours of her body, the bone structure of her face and the pitch of her voice made her a woman. She was not merely 'different' from a man, she was also superior to most men; a manifestly obvious opinion which she held, and took for granted, without needing to voice the fact.

It was possible, more than possible, that she'd had a rough deal in life. That the right man would have contributed to her own blazing personality and made her a gloriously happy woman. So many things were possible. So many things were very probable.

So many things . . .

Therefore Lyle raised an almost cynical eyebrow and murmured, 'His "so-called" respectability?'

She drew on the cigarette, then said, 'He's a local government official. You know that of course?'

'In the treasury department.'

'A senior clerk. A pompous position, held by pompous little men.'

'Not always, surely?' smiled Lyle.

'The exceptions are few.' Her lips moved into a bitter half-smile, but her eyes held veiled contempt. 'They're underpaid, of course they are. But because they hold some degree of responsibility they magnify that responsibility in order to inflate their own petty importance.'

'Bureaucrats,' murmured Lyle.

'Quite. But some of them try to carry their stupid bureaucracies into their home life. George, for example. Unimportant things in themselves, but they add up. I've never known him to wear other than a white shirt. And, whatever the weather, he must wear a tie – a sort of badge of office. Never slippers. I bought him a pair – a birthday present – years ago. They're still in the box. He has a dress – a sort of uniform – and he never doffs it. His suits are dry-cleaned every fortnight. Ritualistic, almost. Every fortnight. Damnation . . .' The mild swear word was like a tiny explosion, then she reverted to her more normal tone, '. . . He never *alters*.'

'Excitement?' said Lyle with a smile.

'No.' She answered carefully. Slowly. She looked around for an ash-tray and Lyle opened a drawer in the table and took out an empty two-ounce St Bruno tobacco tin, removed the lid and placed the tin on the table. She tapped the ash from her cigarette into the tin, then said, 'No, not excitement. Not in that sense. Genuine respectability, I wouldn't mind. Even the restrictive, Victorian kind. If it was genuine.'

'But, of course, the voyeurism?'

'That sickens me,' she admitted. 'If he wants to be a dirty old man, let him get on with it. I wouldn't admire him for it, but I'd tolerate him, perhaps even forgive him. But the other thing. The façade of super-decency, covering peeping Tom antics. That's living a perpetual lie. It's foul. It admits of no possible excuse.'

85

'Mrs Barker.' Lyle leaned forward a little in his chair. He tapped his cigarette gently against the rounded edge of the tobacco tin. In age he was far too young to have been the woman's father, but the voice was paternal; the voice of an age he did not possess, but of a wisdom, based upon experience, she knew nothing about. He said, 'Voyeurism. The – to you, to me – perverted gratification experienced in surreptitiously watching sexual acts. He's not alone. He's not even uncommon. The girlie-girlie magazines. Some of the films, much advertised. Films shown at first-class cinemas. Not the blue films – the reputedly "adult" films. Even some of the television plays. Plays written by established and respected playwrights. Good producers. Fine actors and actresses. First-class camera work. A form of voyeurism . . . surely?'

'I don't buy such magazines. I don't watch that kind of play.'

'Not you, madam. But thousands, hundreds of thousands, do. And not all men. And most certainly not all murderers.'

Lyle watched her face and waited. What he'd said, what his words implied, was too obvious for her not to understand. The kinks, while not yet ruling the world, certainly inhabited the world. And in large numbers. Indeed, there was an argument which insisted that *everybody* was a kink, but that the majority were inhibited, which in turn argued that the kinks were the 'normal' people. A stupid argument, an argument which Lyle refused to use, but an argument much voiced and an argument he was sure she'd heard.

She smoked her cigarette in silence and lived with her indecision.

'You called him a murderer,' he reminded her.

'I did.'

'Do you *still* call him a murderer?'

86

'I do.'

'Why?'

'I – I have my reasons.' Her voice was soft and irresolute.

'Tell me,' he coaxed.

'I've already told you...'

'Nothing, Mrs Barker.' He took a last pull on the cigarette, then squeezed what remained into the bottom of the tobacco tin. 'That he's a peeping Tom. We get a complaint along those lines every week. Into windows. Into parked cars. Frightened men – men who have never reached adulthood – seeking their own brand of kicks. But not murderers. Nobody accuses them of murder. Or of rape. It's a completely different league. Like equating milk-bottle theft with The Great Train Robbery.' In a soft, cajoling tone he said, 'It won't do, madam. Out there, in the Charge Office, you were so certain. So compelling. He's a murderer ... that's what you claim. Now, why is he a murderer? And what makes you so sure?'

CHAPTER NINETEEN

You will, thought Bell, *talk. Already I've gone too far. I'm a dead duck. Half a working lifetime. Crawling through the cesspits of a hundred major criminalities, without once letting the filth touch me. But you! You've cooked me, louse. After this the Civil Liberties mob will have my balls for breakfast. You've done that, bastard. But you'll sing, you foul bloody sparrow, you'll sing.*

That much at least. My job's gone. My pension. Could be I'll end up behind the wall. But you will *talk. And some poor little bitch might live to enjoy life. Some poor kid you'd have taken a fancy to.*

It's a high price, Barker. Your asking price is way and gone to hell beyond what you're worth. But I'll pay it, scum. I'll pay it . . . Willingly.

You may, thought Barker, *kill me. Break bones. Make me scream and yell for mercy. But you're not the one I'm afraid of. Not you . . . the other one. Lyle. He's the one who really frightens me.*

This pain. Very primitive, Sergeant Bell. Very primeval. It won't get you anywhere. A sop to your own masochistic pleasures, perhaps. Masochistic, because you're not an evil man. You're not a sadist. You despise yourself for this abomination – of course you do – and the contempt you have for yourself is your excuse for its continuation. It's unnecessary, and you know it's unnecessary, but you continue because it makes you feel martyrised.

Who knows? ... You may eventually kill me for the sake of your own martyrdom.

As for me? Break me. Smash me. Reduce me to pulp. I deserve it all and more. But to you I will never confess. Never! You are crude, Sergeant Bell — not evil — and crudity sickens me.

CHAPTER TWENTY

'Why a murderer?' asked Lyle.

Edwina Barker was unaware of it, but she was at the receiving end of the very essence of fine detective work. The same question asked, and asked, and asked again. The various answers at first apparently accepted, then analysed and finally rejected. All the excuses – all the explanations – listened to, then quietly shredded and reduced to nothing.

There was no pleasure in what Lyle was doing. No real enjoyment. He was not creating anything . . . except, perhaps, the truth. On the contrary, his task was that of destruction. Subtle destruction. Destruction, guised in a cloak of friendliness, therefore a form of destruction which could be neither seen nor felt. An invisible destruction. But nevertheless a complete destruction.

And Lyle, when he asked the question, 'Why a murderer?' knew that his self-imposed task of clandestine destruction was almost complete.

He held out the opened packet of cigarettes. She took one and lit it from the still-burning stub of the one she was still smoking. Before she could squash the smoked cigarette into the tobacco tin Lyle caught her hand and guided the smouldering end towards his own fresh cigarette. It was a sudden and unexpected physical contact. In some strange way, intimate. In some strange way, secret. It seemed to seal a bond between them; to set them apart from the rest of the world . . . as close and as isolated as lovers.

He released her hand and she screwed the used cigarette into the tobacco tin.

'Well?' he asked.

She told it as if talking to herself. Like a stumbling monologue, and yet a monologue well-learned, as if she'd repeated the story a hundred times before and in the same words. Yet stumbling and unable to find the appropriate words or, if finding them – if knowing them – unable to voice them. Revealing herself – revealing her inner self – and, with the shedding of each veil, trembling a little more as if with cold; as if the shame and humiliation contained an invisible refrigerative element beyond the warming capacity of any external heat.

She said, 'Five years ago . . . Six years ago, perhaps. How long ago doesn't matter. I have a brother . . . A married brother and – and it was Christmas. A Christmas party. On the Boxing Day. In – in Sheffield. That's where he lives. He and his wife. And his daughter. A little girl. A very – a very beautiful little girl. Cindy. I – I love her dearly. I – I think she loves me, too. I hope so. She deserves to be loved. Some children . . . they have magic. A touch of magic about them. An – an innocence. A sweetness. Some children have it. Cindy has it.

'She's twelve years old now. Twelve. And it was five – perhaps six – Christmases ago. A party on Boxing Day. Just a small party. My brother and his wife. George. Me. And – and Cindy. Quiet. Not a rowdy party. We – we don't drink much. Nobody was drunk. Nobody can blame drink for what happened. We'd – we'd had a nice day. Exchanging presents. W-watching the television. Helping Cindy play with her toys. Talking. That's all. That sort of thing. That – that sort of party. Just – just the five of us.

'We'd – we'd had tea. A lovely tea. Ham . . . cold ham they'd boiled themselves. I don't think I've ever tasted better . . . And – and lettuce and a whole salad – a lovely salad – it must have taken her hours to prepare. My brother's wife, I mean. And – and trifle, with real cream, and Christmas cake, and mince pies, and – and – and . . .

'It – it was a wonderful meal. And we were all so happy. Happy. Really happy. Like – like a family should be at Christmas. Happy and warm and feeling good. Like – like a Christmas. A real Christmas. And – and the men had had cigars. After the meal, I mean. Cigars. And my sister-in-law and I had smoked cigarettes. Too many cigarettes . . . you always smoke too many cigarettes at Christmas, don't you? And – and Cindy. Somebody had bought her some pretend cigarettes. Sweets, really. But they looked a little like real cigarettes. And – and she was pretending to be grown up. Smoking a pretend cigarette, while her mummy and I smoked real cigarettes. While – while George and her daddy smoked cigars. It was – it was . . . so happy.

'Then – then we had to wash the crockery. My sister-in-law and I. We were washing up. The crockery. The cutlery. We'd – we'd had this lovely meal and we were clearing away. Into the kitchen to do – to do the washing-up. I remember the tea service. A Christmas present to my sister-in-law from her husband. Beautiful. Tiny pink roses. A pattern of tiny . . . And I was so afraid I might break one of them. I – I carried them so carefully. From the dining room to the kitchen. It would have spoiled everything if I'd . . .

'And Bill – that's my brother – Bill . . . Wilfred, really. But he never liked "Wilf" . . . so we shortened it to "Bill". Bill was upstairs. He has a . . . He's one of those hi-fi enthusiasts. He was upstairs. Carols, I think. Or was it Bach's Christmas Oratorio? I – I think it was the oratorio. We'd had the carols. Yes – because we never got round to the . . . Anyway, he was upstairs looking for a recording of Bach's Christmas Oratorio. I'm – I'm sure it was the oratorio. And we – Alice and I – were in the kitchen. Washing up. That left – that left George and Cindy in the dining room. Alone.'

She stopped. The big hurdle was ahead of her. Only that one big hurdle left and although she'd scaled it every day – every night – in the privacy of her tormented mind, she'd never before scaled it publicly and in the presence of a stranger. It was too late to stop; she'd already said too much. It had to be told and she had to tell it, but it was perhaps the most difficult thing she'd ever done in her life.

She drew on the cigarette. Deep and long. She exhaled the smoke, then continued in a voice pitched slightly lower – slightly softer – than before.

'The side-plates. We'd used five side-plates. Five of us . . . so we'd used five side-plates. And – and I'd only brought four from the dining room. I – I thought I'd brought them all. But I'd only brought four. So – so – so I went back into the dining room. A lot of – of wrapping paper around. Christmas paper. What we'd wrapped the presents in. I thought – I thought the side-plate might be . . .

'He was there. George. Still – still on the dining chair. Turned away from the table. And – and Cindy was on his knee. And he had his hand . . . She was wearing a lovely scarlet dress. Trimmed with white imitation fur. Santa Claus. We'd – we'd called it her "Santa Claus" dress. Such a pretty dress. Alice had made it for her. For Christmas. And – and – and . . .' It was almost a groan, as she said, 'He had his hand under the hem of the dress. Under the fur. His – his whole hand. His whole forearm. And – the *animal* – with his other hand he was guiding Cindy's hand . . . He was – he was unzipped. And he was – was – was . . .'

She broke. The tears spilled from her eyes and rolled

down her cheeks. She stared at Lyle's face, but couldn't focus for the tears. She pleaded, 'Do I have to . . . ? Must I go on?'

'No,' said Lyle, gently.

'That child. That poor child.' She dropped her head, took a tiny, lace-fringed handkerchief from the pocket of her two-piece, wiped her eyes and blew her nose. In a fractionally more controlled voice she said, 'I saw the child. Cindy. I saw her face. And she *knew*. She was frightened . . . terrified. But, you see, it was her uncle. Her uncle George. So – although she knew something was wrong – she didn't know what . . . but, her uncle George. Uncles don't – don't . . .' Once more she paused, swallowed, drew hard on the cigarette then in a firm voice said, 'That's it, inspector. He's a child-rapist. And a child-murderer. Never doubt it for a moment.'

CHAPTER TWENTY-ONE

Bell had Barker's tie and shirt-front in a tight-clenched grip. The balled fist of his right hand was already drawn back for the first punishing blow.

It was as close as *that* when the door opened and the uniformed constable entered the room and said, 'The tea's brew – ' His eyes widened and he gasped. 'For Christ's sake!' Then he bawled, '*Sergeant!*'

Bell's voice was ugly with the rasp of frustrated anger as he snarled, 'Why the bloody hell couldn't you have ... ?'

'*Sergeant! Have you a minute, please?*'

The uniformed constable was not addressing Detective Sergeant Bell. The uniformed constable was in at the deep end and knew it. He was out of his depth – well out of his depth – and was, in effect, screaming for a life-line. He held the door wide and took his eyes off Bell and Barker only long enough to turn his head and direct his yell for assistance along the corridor and in the general direction of the Charge Office.

Bell lowered his fist and unclenched his fingers from the front of Barker's shirt. He stepped away from the frightened Barker and directed a look of fathomless contempt at the slightly panic-stricken uniformed constable.

He said, 'Of all the gutless slobs. Of all the ...'

'I'm sorry, sergeant.' This time the uniformed constable was addressing Bell. 'I want none of this. This makes me a witness, right? And a witness to summat I don't like.'

'Two to one,' said Bell, savagely.

'Aye.' The uniformed constable nodded. 'Two to one if I lie. Two to one if I tell the truth. Sorry. I wouldn't lie for you, Sergeant Bell. I wouldn't lie about this for anybody.'

The office-duty sergeant arrived. He needed no explanation. One swift scan round the room and he knew what has happening and what had happened. His jaw hardened, he jerked his head and said, 'Outside, lad.'

'With pleasure, sergeant.' The uniformed constable hurried into the corridor and away towards the Charge Office.

'You, too, Bell,' said the office-duty sergeant. Bell made as if to argue and the office-duty sergeant thrust out his jaw, and repeated, 'You, too, Bell. Don't arse things up more than you have already. And shut the door behind you.'

Bell hesitated. Then, quite suddenly, he seemed to deflate; to shrink and fold in upon himself. To lose all the spit and sparkle which was part of his personality. He walked across the room and, had he been a dog, his tail would have been between his legs. Not, be it understood, because he was afraid of the office-duty sergeant. Rather because he was suddenly conscious of exactly what he'd done; of the fact that he, and his family, were out on the loneliest limb in the world. That, thanks to the passionate hatred he held for all Barker stood for, he'd smashed everything. His job. His future. Perhaps even his liberty.

He closed the door quietly and left the office-duty sergeant and Barker alone in the room.

The office-duty sergeant stood for a moment looking at Barker in silence. Then he said, 'My name's Adams.'

Barker moved his head in a tiny jerk of acknowledgement. Much of the terror had gone from his expression, but a residue of fear and puzzlement remained. Who was this man, Adams, anyway? One of 'them'? But of course he was one of 'them'. He wore the uniform and the badges of rank. He was the enemy.

And yet, although the enemy, he might have honour. The man, Lyle, had honour. A form of 'official' decency. This man, too, perhaps.

Adams said, 'Smack you in the mouth, did he?'

'No,' muttered Barker.

'Your mouth's bleeding. He must have . . .'

'It's where I bit into my lip. I wasn't going to give him the pleasure of . . .'

Barker's voice trailed off into silence. As if he was tired. Weary of fighting a battle he knew he couldn't win.

Adams glanced at the corner of the room and said, 'There's soap and water over there. Hot water. And a towel. Clean yourself up a bit. You'll feel better.'

Barker hauled himself from the chair. He walked toward the wash-basin. Doubled up slightly, and still in some pain.

'The guts?' asked Adams, bluntly.

'And the back,' mumbled Barker.

'Need a doctor?'

'No.'

'Don't be too stuck-up, lad. If you think you need a doctor, just say so.'

'I don't need a doctor.' There was a touch of savage determination in Barker's tone.

As Barker washed his hands and face and rinsed his mouth with cold water Adams hitched a buttock onto a corner of the table and talked. His voice was very matter-of-fact. Neither coaxing, nor threatening. Just a man talking to another man.

He said, 'They say we close ranks. Y'know, summat like this happens and we close ranks and do a cover-up job, that's what some of 'em say. They're wrong. They couldn't be more wrong. I've seen you. I dunno what happened, but I can guess. I know what you looked like when I arrived here. I'll stand witness, if necessary. He'd no right. I know it – you know it – I'll stand witness.'

Adams began to swing his free leg. Slowly. Gently. In time with his words.

He said, 'Bell. This is summat new for him. A bit of a one-man commando unit, sometimes. He likes a scrap. But not this. This is summat new. To knock a prisoner around. I've never known him do it before. It's a new departure.

'I think there's a reason and I think I know the reason. He's married. Two kids. Both girls. One's coming up to six. The elder's just past eight. The right age . . . see? Standish. Wallace. Roberts. All of an age. Roughly the same age as Bell's kids. I reckon his imagination got the better of him. It shouldn't. It's no excuse. Objectivity, that's what we're supposed to have. Complete objectivity. But sometimes it's not easy. Sometimes . . .'

'It doesn't matter.' Barker cupped his hands under the tap, sucked water past his lips, then spat the pink-stained water into the wash-basin. He said, 'It doesn't matter at all.'

'You have a complaint,' said Adams.

'It's nothing.' Adams dried his mouth and hands on the towel. 'Compared with the other thing. It's nothing.'

'It's your decision, Barker.'

'It's nothing. I don't want to make a complaint. He was doing his job – what he *thought* was his job – and thinking of his own little girls. I don't blame him.'

'I'll tell him.' Adams slipped to his feet, unbuttoned one of the breast pockets of his uniform, took out a comb and held it towards Barker. Barker ignored Adams's comb, walked to the table, picked up his own comb and ran it through his hair. Adams added, 'He'll – er – he'll want to thank you. I'll tell him.'

'Bell?'

'Aye.' Adams returned his comb to his pocket.

Barker walked to the mirror to straighten his tie. With

98

his back to Adams he said, 'I don't want to see him again.'

'Look, he'll want to . . .'

'Do I have a choice?' Barker turned from the mirror. 'I'm under arrest. I know that limits my freedom of action, but I don't want to see Bell again. If I do I might feel inclined to change my mind.'

'Y'mean make a complaint?'

'After what he's done to me, I might very easily change my mind.' Barker dusted his soiled trousers and jacket with the palms of his hands. 'It's up to you. It's up to him.'

'Aye.' Adams's grunt meant nothing whatever.

Barker walked back to the chair. Apart from an occasional wince as a stab of pain caught him he walked quite normally.

He said, 'You might tell Inspector Lyle, please.'

'Aye . . . I'll do that.'

'And ask him – as a favour – if you can be spared.'

'Me?' Adams frowned.

'To take notes. Presumably notes will have to be taken.'

'Somebody'll have to take 'em,' agreed Adams.

'If I have a choice, I prefer you. But not Bell . . . anybody rather than Bell.'

'I'll tell him,' said Adams, solemnly. As he opened the door, he added, 'I'll send the constable back. I'll get him to fix you up with a cuppa.'

As he walked along the corridor towards the Charge Office, Adams blew out his cheeks, then grinned to himself. He'd pulled it again. The old 'Ways and Means Act'. Christ, they should give him a medal. But he'd pulled it. Old Charlie Bell, right up the creek in a barbed-wire canoe. *And* without a paddle in sight. What the steaming hell had made him run berserk? And with a louse like Barker? The Barkers of the world weren't worth the risk . . . ever.

99

Still, never mind, eh?

All that crap about Bell's 'little girls'. May the good Lord forgive him. The truth was that Bell had a duo of strapping great sons; one in his late teens, the other in his early twenties. One was on his way to becoming an accountant. The other was nearing the end of his training as a veterinary surgeon. And either one of 'em could have torn one of Barker's arms off its hinges and beaten him over the head with it.

Well, so what?

Barker didn't know. It was doubtful if he'd ever know. And if he did eventually get to know it would be too late. Long gone too late to start bleating about 'police violence'. As for the blinder about 'little girls', that would boil down to a straight Barker versus Adams face-out and Barker wouldn't have a sniff of a chance.

The old 'Ways and Means' ...

Nevertheless, he'd have to have a word with Charlie Bell *and* put Lyle in the picture.

CHAPTER TWENTY-TWO

Something about 'a trouble shared'. There was a great truth in it. Lyle made a calculated guess; that this was the first time Edwina Barker had talked to a stranger about the incident of a few Christmases ago. And she looked better for it. More relaxed. Less brittle and, in some strange way, *relieved*. The tiny muscles of her face were less taut and this in turn lent her expression a more soft look.

They were into their third cigarette and Lyle said, 'Divorce? At a guess I'd say the incident with Cindy would have formed a basis. But – I take it – you didn't give it serious consideration?'

'I wish I could have.' She smiled and, this time, the smile carried something other than bitterness. A touch of impishness perhaps. She said, 'That would have given his precious "respectability" a nasty jolt.'

'Indeed.'

'But, you probably know, it might have meant Cindy giving evidence. He'd have fought the petition. I know him too well to have any doubts about that. And Cindy . . . I couldn't possibly have allowed her to explain – *try* to explain – what he'd done. Best forgotten as far as she was concerned.'

'But you still lived with him?' probed Lyle, gently.

'Inspector Lyle.' Again the smile. This time a slow, wry smile of accepted fate. 'Don't believe all you hear about the "liberated woman". Most women are like me. Married, which means tied. Being a housewife remains "unskilled labour". Oh, I know, you see adverts for "housekeepers" in the newspapers. But so often it's the same thing, but without the security of a marriage certificate. George can't sack me. I have that comfort. I also have a home which is *my* home. The physical side of marriage? I can't talk about men but, if a woman decides to make that part of marriage unimportant, it *becomes* unimportant. Mind over matter I suppose. I – er – I have no right to refuse him. But I can make it repellent. A score of quite deliberate ploys, inspector. Every woman knows them. Played properly they can make a man feel unclean. In time, I'm told, they can even make him impotent.'

'You've – er – you've repaid him,' murmured Lyle.

'And will for the rest of my life.'

'Just one thing . . .' Lyle gave the impression of musing aloud. It was more of a hypothetical proposition than a question. 'Three kids have been murdered. Raped, then murdered. It could be argued that the man responsible – whoever he is – was grabbing at forbidden fruit, because the fruit to which he had claim was being denied him.'

'Little girls?' For the first time since she'd unburdened herself, her lips curled into a leisurely sneer.

'A coward?' suggested Lyle.

'He's certainly that,' she agreed.

'Well?'

A tiny word. A nothing. A word thrown, haphazardly, into normal conversation, like so much verbal confetti. One of the oral sweetmeats of the English language. But this time and in quiet question form like a tiny fire-cracker exploding in the confined space of the Interview Room.

'Oh, my God!' she breathed. The colour left her face and she drew on her cigarette, and the spiral of smoke from the glowing tobacco magnified the slight tremble of her hand. Then she whispered, 'Oh, my God! If I've been indirectly responsible.'

'I wouldn't know,' said Lyle blandly.

'You've just said . . .'

'A possible argument. No more.'

She hung her head as if in shame, then muttered, 'I'd hate to be married to you, inspector.'

Lyle smiled and said, 'I don't make those sort of snap judgements, Mrs Barker.'

'You know how to drive the knife home. That's what I mean. And give it that little twist which really hurts.'

'You're the one who called him a murderer. Who was so sure.'

'And he isn't?' She raised her head and pleaded with her eyes.

'A court will decide . . . eventually.'

'No. I mean you. What do *you* think?'

'I think you're right,' said Lyle calmly. Ruthlessly. 'I think he *is* the murderer. The rapist. The court may find him innocent. An acquittal. Who knows? Anything's possible in a court of law. But that won't alter my opinion . . . or yours.'

The silence was interrupted by a tap on the Interview Room door.

Lyle called, 'Come in.'

The uniformed constable entered. He was carrying a cheap tin tray upon which were cups of tea and a tiny plate holding biscuits.

As he placed the tray on the table he said, 'With the compliments of Sergeant Adams, sir. And will you have a word with him as soon as it's convenient.'

CHAPTER TWENTY-THREE

'Away home, Charlie,' advised Adams. 'Sleep on it. If there's trouble it'll still be here, come morning. Waiting for you.'

'There'll be trouble,' said Bell, glumly.

'Not as I read the signs. We keep it from the chief inspector, we're in the clear.'

'Can we?' Bell sounded very doubtful.

'He's a very conscientious type.' Adams blew down the stem of an ancient pipe to check the air-way. He took a pouch from his tunic pocket and, as he talked, he fingered shredded tobacco into the bowl of the pipe. 'It's . . .' He glanced up at the wall clock. '. . . five-past one. He'll be on the street till two. Very conscientious. Keeps the lads on their toes. That's his motto. By then I'll have had a word with Lyle. Lyle's no book man, not at the bottom of him. Come tomorrow he'll have mulled things over and seen the light. He'll probably chew your balls off, but what if he does? You'll still have a job and a pension. That's the main thing.'

Had anybody accused Adams of 'closing the ranks' – of 'doing a cover-up job' – he would have strenuously denied that accusation. He was, by *his* yardstick, merely being practical. Barker had had his opportunity; he could have howled the place down and made an official complaint. And he'd have been well within his rights. Fine. But those 'rights' had a reverse side, too. The right *not* to make a complaint; to believe, if he so wished, a fairy story concerning two non-existent daughters of Bell and to place those fictitious kids in the pans of the balance and decide accordingly.

The man was a killer, and a killer of the worst kind. Start with that proposition and what Bell had done to him amounted to damn-all. Barker knew this. Barker was also something of a mug; just look at Charlie Bell and do your basic arithmetic. He had neither the age (or should it be youth?) nor the build, to suggest that some young raver might throw herself on her back for the sole purpose of *his* carnal pleasure. As sure as hell he hadn't the money; detectives (even detective sergeants) did not kick up their heels with the jet set. A man well into the middle-age stakes. A man with a bay-window belly. A man with a lot of grey in his hair. And a six-year-old and an eight-year-old?

Okay, it was possible, but to suck *that* lemon without even looking at the skin made Barker something very much of a mug.

Adams had a crystal-clear conscience and saw no reason for it to be otherwise. Bell on the other hand was worried.

In the first place he lacked the simple, uncomplicated gall of Adams. He had, to use the more modern terminology, 'lost his cool' and moreover lost it in a big way. It had been very nice kicking hell out of that bastard Barker. Wrong, uncalled for, illegal and the action of a lout. All these things . . . but very nice.

Except that in retrospect it was also very nasty. Nasty and nice, both at the same time. Bell was on a see-saw he couldn't control and that Adams had temporarily steadied that see-saw gave him small comfort.

And as if to make matters worse, as if to rub it in, they were in the deserted C.I.D. Office. Their conversation was of a very confidential nature and Adams had suggested the C.I.D. Office for maximum privacy.

Fine, except that the C.I.D. Office brought back memories.

In the past and via the men who used these now empty

desks he, Bell, had organised some very neat little man-hunts. Detection had been the name of the game and he'd captained a very good team. Good lads, every one of 'em. He liked 'em and up to now they'd all liked him. No clock-watching. No tantrums. No arguments. Between them they had a track record second to none.

Jesus Christ!

He knew every scratch-mark on every desk. That damn radiator, the one under the far window on the left, it *always* had an air-lock. Every other radiator gave off heat, while that one stayed as cold as a nun's kiss. Even the typewriters. That old Imperial; would it hell as space properly . . . not since some clumsy bugger had dropped it on the floor. It was never used. It was always kept under wraps. But it had to *be* here because it was on the inventory and because requisitioning for a new typewriter would make the store wallahs blow blue steam and ask a lot of awkward questions.

Jesus Christ!

So many memories . . . and he'd done a real demolition job on the lot of 'em, just because Barker had got up his nostrils.

Adams puffed at his pipe for a moment, then removed it from his mouth, and said, 'Charlie, for God's sake go home. You're driving yourself nuts.'

Bell muttered, 'I maybe should go in to Barker and . . .'

'He'll blow the whistle if he sees you,' interrupted Adams. 'He means it.'

'Oh, my Christ!'

'Forget it, Charlie. We all make mistakes. You've had your quota for today. Now go home.'

Bell sighed and said, 'Maybe.'

'I'll ring you if anything develops,' promised Adams.

Bell nodded defeat and moved towards the door of the C.I.D. Office with all the weariness of a defeated man.

CHAPTER TWENTY-FOUR

In the Interview Room Edwina Barker sipped half-cold, over-sweetened tea, smoked yet another cigarette and played touch-me-if-you-dare with alarming thoughts.

Lyle granted her the silence in which to torture herself.

And what, she thought, *if what this man suggests is true? What if I am indirectly responsible for the ravishing of three tiny bodies? For the snuffing out of three innocent lives?*

It can't be. It mustn't be!

It's devil's advocacy carried to an illogical conclusion. Carried too far, much too far. The same road would end up by arguing that my own mother was equally indirectly responsible, because she gave birth to me. That she taught me my values. Or that her mother gave birth to her, and taught her values. It's a never-ending argument. It becomes ridiculous. It is ridiculous.

George is the guilty one. Nobody else. He shares the guilt with no other person on earth.

And yet . . .

Call him an animal. Call his carnality bestial. Call him a fornicator. And having called him all these things — and believing all these things — where does that leave me?

I'm his wife. I took certain vows. I stood before an altar — before God — and made solemn promises. 'For better, for worse.' And that must include everything. It includes everything or it includes nothing, therefore it includes everything. Up to and including being the willing vessel for his intemperate lust.

And if I am not? If I refuse? . . . as I have refused?

And if he cannot control this intemperate lust of his?

She lowered the cup to the saucer. It made a tiny rattle before it came to final rest.

Lyle looked at her questioningly.

'I'd – I'd like to go home, inspector,' she said hoarsely.

'Of course.' Lyle stood up, then held her chair as she rose to her feet. He said, 'I'll arrange for transport.'

'No, I think I need the walk.'

'It's after one,' said Lyle. 'Not the safest time of the day to be walking the streets. I'll have somebody accompany you.'

'No.' She moved past him towards the door which he held open. 'To walk alone, please. To – to think a little, perhaps more than a little.'

CHAPTER TWENTY-FIVE

And in the room which was a multi-purpose room there, too, there was a silence, fat and bloated with unspoken thoughts.

The uniformed constable had resumed his position on the chair by the door. His expression suggested that he was in something of a quandary. Awkward and more than a little embarrassed. His brows were lowered in a half-scowl and he kept his eyes fixed on a spot on the lino, about two yards in front of his feet. He wished to heavens Lyle or Adams, or even Bell, would come back and relieve him of a responsibility which, to tell the truth, he neither wanted nor understood.

At the table Barker sat and (unknowingly, but like his wife) sipped at tasteless tea and smoked a cigarette. Occasionally he rubbed his spine with his left hand. Much of the pain had dissipated into a dull ache, but there was this one spot. Tender to the touch and, at a guess, already discoloured.

Deserved? He asked himself. *Not allowed, of course. Nobody had made pretence that what Bell had done was other than illegal. But, legalities apart,* deserved?

He supposed so. There was so much 'wrong' with him. Such a great warping of normal standards of simple decency. It wasn't that he was consciously evil. Not even consciously 'different'. Just weak. And, of course, driven to distraction by Edwina's steely refusal to even try to understand.

The self-pity swelled and threatened to choke him. It

filled the tear ducts behind his eyes and almost spilled over.

Why, thought Barker, *hasn't somebody helped me? Why hasn't somebody seen me as I truly am? A man with a problem. Like a cleft palate or a squint. That sort of problem. Something I was born with. Something I can't control. Something for which I'm not responsible.*

My wife, my brother in-law, my sister-in-law . . . they all loathe me. I disgust them and, the truth is, I understand their feeling of disgust. Cindy is afraid of me. Her uncle, and she is afraid of me. She doesn't know why she is afraid. She has merely been taught to be afraid. Never to be alone with 'Uncle George'. What horrors that must conjure up in her young mind. What terrifying imagining.

All this. All the other things. And now my reason for being here, arrested for triple rape and triple murder.

Why has nobody yet tried to understand me? To help me? To dig into my brain and root out this twisted thing of which I am so ashamed? Why haven't they helped me?

WHY HAVEN'T THEY EVER HELPED ME?

CHAPTER TWENTY-SIX

Lyle was not a man to be angry. Such men are never truly angry; they pretend anger when the pretence is necessary; they play-act anger if such play-acting is called for and, when they do so, their expertise is such that few outsiders can identify it as mock-emotion. Anger is to such men a completely non-productive luxury. It blinds. It serves no useful purpose whatever. It clutters the brain and builds a wall behind which the truth can easily hide.

They use make-believe as it suits them. To frighten perhaps. To emphasise a point of argument, or to demolish an opposition. But, for whatever reason, they use this paste emotion and, unlike more normal men, they control *it*, rather than *it* controlling them.

Lyle, then, was not angry. He was surprised and, to a degree, disappointed; disappointed that a man holding the rank of detective sergeant had not, long ago, recognised anger as a stupidity and removed it from his make-up.

He tapped the nail of his left thumb with his folded, half-moon spectacles and said, 'Stupid and quite uncalled for. And quite unnecessary.'

'Yes, sir,' said Adams, solemnly.

They were in the corridor, mid-way between the Charge Office and the room in which Barker waited. They talked in hushed tones. Like conspirators, which in fact they were.

'The chief inspector . . .' began Lyle.

'He's still on the streets,' interrupted Adams. 'He'll be in soon for supper. Soon. But not yet.'

'When *he's* told . . .'

'Need he be told?' asked Adams innocently.

'He carries the senior rank, sergeant. That means he carries the final responsibility.'

'For what he knows,' argued Adams gently. 'What he doesn't know, he can't be responsible for.'

'That's a fallacious argument, Sergeant Adams. One the powers-that-be won't accept.'

'If *they* ever get to know,' teased Adams.

Lyle tapped the thumb-nail musingly for a moment, then he said, 'It's an argument, also, for blackmail of course. If we keep it to ourselves you can blackmail me. I can blackmail you. Barker can blackmail us all. We'll be playing with fire.'

'Barker's already on fire . . . and knows it.' Adams grinned. 'And who blackmails friends?'

Lyle said, 'Don't take Barker too much for granted, sergeant. He's in a corner, but he's still capable of fighting back.'

'From what Bell said . . .'

'Oh, he'll crack.' Lyle stopped tapping the thumb-nail with the folded spectacles and instead rested them against his chin. He said, 'The problem isn't getting him to crack. We can prove him a liar half-a-dozen times over on what he's already said and that, alone, should open the flood-gates. But I want more than that. I want an itemised statement. Volunteered by him and without even a suggestion on our part. That's what I want. I might not get it. But I want as much of it as possible. I want him inside *my* box . . . nailed, screwed, glued and dovetailed.'

'Try it,' suggested Adams invitingly. 'Your way. I'll not do a Charlie Bell on you. Just take it from the top, as it comes, and make up your mind about the other thing later. Just give it a spin, sir, eh?'

Lyle tapped his chin a couple of times with the folded

spectacles. A contemplative movement; as if he'd already reached a decision and was only encircling that decision in order to examine it from as many angles as possible in order to carefully count the weaknesses and the possible loopholes.

Then, he said, 'Arrange things, sergeant. I'll check through Bell's notes. Tell the men in the Charge Office where you are and make some sort of excuse for Sergeant Bell's absence – for the benefit of the chief inspector. As you say, we'll give it a spin.'

CHAPTER TWENTY-SEVEN

The concept of time, itself, dying. A proposition beyond the bounds of visualisation, perhaps, something outside the reach of ordinary imagination. One day some skilled writer of science fiction will take this 'impossible' concept and use it as a base for some theory which in time the less imaginative scientists of the world will prove to be true. That time, itself, *does* die.

But every copper who ever worked a night-shift needs no scientific formula upon which to build this (but not to him) 'impossible' proposition. Time dies once every twenty-four hours and the time of its death is at, or around, 2 a.m. Its death can be felt on the streets, especially on the cold streets of winter. The damp and deserted streets; the echoing, darkened and strangely narrowed streets. There time has, momentarily, died. The momentous death is also felt within every police station and at the same hour. The teleprinter clacks and whirs in a vacuum without beginning and without end; its messages are, for that moment, meaningless and as from another universe.

Then life once more takes up its pulse and once more lives. But in a weakened state. Slow and, or so it would seem, unwilling to live until one more dawn quickens its heart-beat, warms its blood and hurries it towards its next daily death.

Lyle knew all about the 2 a.m. syndrome. It was an experience he had often suffered, but never come to enjoy. He placed his elbows on the table, cupped his face in the palms of his hands and pressed his fingers against his eyes.

He lowered his hands, took the handkerchief from his pocket and began to polish the lenses of his spectacles.

Almost off-handedly, he remarked, 'You have, of course, cause for complaint.'

'Sir?' The lethargy which had also embraced Barker was blinked aside and he frowned non-understanding at the detective inspector.

'I'm told . . .' Lyle continued polishing the lenses. '. . . Sergeant Bell has assaulted you in my absence.'

On the chair, by the door, Adams mentally crossed his fingers.

Barker said, 'He lost his temper.'

'A poor excuse.' Lyle returned the handkerchief to his pocket and hooked the spectacles over his ears.

'I don't blame him,' said Barker.

'Really?'

'If he seriously thinks I'm guilty of – of . . .' Barker moved his shoulders and left the sentence unfinished.

'Quite.' Lyle straightened the contents of the envelope-files. 'Nevertheless, you have cause for complaint.'

'It doesn't matter.'

'Meaning you won't complain?'

'Meaning I won't complain,' said Barker.

Adams mentally uncrossed his fingers and prepared himself for taking notes.

Lyle squared the papers in one of the envelope-files and said, 'We'll start where we left off, shall we, Mr Barker? I think we'd . . .'

'My wife,' interrupted Barker.

Lyle raised his eyebrows and gazed, with puzzled curiosity, over the half-moon lenses and at the face of his antagonist.

'She's on her way home,' he murmured.

'No. I mean what did she say?'

'Oh, many things,' said Lyle, airily. 'A great many things. Very interesting things.'

'About me?'

'Naturally.'

'What, for example?'

Lyle moved his hands to the corners of the table. He stiffened his arms, raised his head and looked down the table at Barker. Each movement was deliberate – almost slow-motion – and a silent taunt at this new and frightening ignorance, on the part of Barker.

He said, 'Correct me if I'm wrong, Mr Barker. But as I recall you refused to see her.'

'Yes, but . . .'

'You refused to allow her to see you.'

'I know, but . . .'

'Nobody said you couldn't. Nobody said you shouldn't. The choice was yours, it was a free choice and you were very dogmatic. Isn't that right?'

'Yes, but . . .'

'You could have been present. You could have heard every word she said. Every question I asked. You chose not to.' Lyle shook his head and smiled. He said, 'I'm sorry, Mr Barker. You can't have the penny *and* the bun, now can you?'

For a moment they stared into each other's eyes. A tiny clash of wills.

Then Barker lowered his gaze and muttered, 'It was all lies, anyway.'

'Probably,' agreed Lyle mildly.

'But you'll believe her.'

Lyle said, 'I try not to believe lies, Mr Barker. Whoever tells them. I try to find the truth . . . assuming there is such a thing.' He removed his hands from the corner of the table, sorted through the documents in one of the envelope-files, then said, 'Now, if we may, let's go back to the evening of the third. When, as you say, you found the murdered body of the Roberts girl.'

'I've already told you everything...'

'No. Not quite everything.' Lyle held up a gently admonishing finger. 'For example. You say you recognised her.'

'Ye-es.'

'Now, let me get the picture properly painted, Mr Barker. As you tell it, of course.' Lyle gazed at a far corner of the room's ceiling and, in a sing-song tone, said, 'You're there on the common. Alone except for the dog, Spot. You're there. The dog's running around, enjoying himself. You're just stretching your legs . . . presumably. Enjoying yourself in your own quiet way . . . presumably. It wasn't a bad evening. Better than the day had been in fact. A little rain during the day, as I recall. But the evening turned clear and, apart from a slight nip in the air, a very pleasant evening. Just the sort of weather to take a dog for a run. Am I right, so far?'

Barker nodded.

'Good. That much, then, is the truth . . . probably. The walk. The dog. The common. Specifics, which we are entitled to take for granted. But why the ditch?'

'The . . .' Barker swallowed. 'Ditch?'

'Where the body was. It had rained during the day, remember? Ditches are messy places at the best of times. Even when it hasn't rained for weeks. Very messy. And messy for some yards on either side more often than not. This one was no exception. The whole common to go at and you end up in the ditch. Why?'

'I – I – I . . . The body.'

'Oh, no. Not from the common. Long grass. Long, dead grass and lots of old, dead leaves. I've *seen* the place, Mr Barker. The body was virtually invisible from the common. And yet you found it . . . or so you claim.'

'I'm – I'm sorry,' stumbled Barker.

'Sorry?'

'I – I don't follow your line of argument. I'm sorry.'

'I think you do, Mr Barker.' Lyle smiled pleasantly. He leaned forward over the table and drew invisible rings and lines on the polished surface with a forefinger. 'There . . . the common. There . . . the ditch in which the body was found. And there – separated from the common by the ditch – the coppice. You know the coppice, of course?'

Barker nodded.

Lyle intoned, 'Dead leaves in the ditch. Dead leaves means trees. Very few trees on commons. No trees at all on *this* common. Therefore the leaves come from the trees of the coppice.' He stabbed the polished surface once more and ended, 'There . . . the body of Gwendolen Roberts.'

Barker remained silent.

'You're with me so far?' said Lyle, mildly.

'Yes.'

'Were you walking along the ditch?' asked Lyle. 'By that, I mean in the ditch? Along the run of the ditch?'

'No. Of course not. You'd need Wellington boots to . . .'

'My point precisely.' Lyle leaned back from the table. 'Therefore you must have been *crossing* the ditch. From the common to the coppice or from the coppice to the common. Which?'

'Why should I cross the . . . ?'

'Please tell *me*,' interrupted Lyle politely.

'Why should I cross the ditch?' Barker repeated and completed his previous question.

'To get to the coppice or to return *from* the coppice, obviously.'

'I – I don't know what you're getting at.'

'Going to? Or coming from?'

The technique was to ignore Barker's professed non-understanding; to treat this pseudo-ignorance as a mere means of gaining time.

Interviews – especially prolonged interviews – have these key moments. The interviewee is forced into a position of non-retraction and, at that point, and however much he ducks and sways, he is cornered. He must, if not always show himself up as a liar, at least tacitly acknowledge that the complete truth has not yet been told. To an outsider it may mean little, a mere insignificance, far too weak to carry any real accusation. But to the interviewer and to the interviewee it represents a break-through. The first flaw upon the surface of the pillar of outraged guiltlessness. Some slight variation upon the 'it-wasn't-me' theme.

'Going to? Or coming from?'

Having given Barker ample time in which to answer Lyle repeated the question. Softly. Invitingly. Requiring an answer, however long he had to wait.

'Come . . .' Barker seemed to choke on the words, then whispered, 'Coming from.'

'Coming from the coppice?'

Barker nodded.

'Good.' Lyle smiled. A friendly smile. A happy smile. A satisfied smile. He said, 'Fine. That's another step forward, isn't it?' He waved a hand at Barker's packet of cigarettes. 'Have a smoke. It might quieten your nerves a little.'

CHAPTER TWENTY-EIGHT

Beautiful, thought Adams. *Bloody magnificent! He's got him into the coppice. He can't 'come away from' without having been there. And that's where the assault and the killing took place. In the coppice.*

Something we know. Something the general public haven't yet been told. But – bet your boots! – something Barker knows.

And that last bit . . .

'It might quieten your nerves.' Sweet. Sweet as a nut, Lyle, old cock. Like a dentist saying, 'This won't hurt a bit,' when he knows – and you know – it's going to hurt like merry hell. The fine and gentle art of subtle kidology.

Damn you, thought Barker. *Damn you for the most foxy creature on God's earth, Inspector Lyle.*

Bell I could tolerate. The boot, the fist, the physical pain. That was nothing. Nothing! From now till dawn and Bell wouldn't have beaten that admission from me. Three men have already questioned me and they haven't had even a hint of what you've just made me say.

But you, Inspector Lyle, you know of my guilt. You know of my secret and, to you, it is no secret. You know. You are aware. And, God help me, you might – you just might – force a confession from me . . . if only to rid myself of you!

CHAPTER TWENTY-NINE

Barker took a cigarette from the packet. He closed the packet then, as if remembering something, re-opened the packet and held it out to Lyle. It was an odd sequence of tiny events. It seemed to say something. A compliance, perhaps. A yielding; the acceptance of a defeat. Not the final defeat, but a defeat nevertheless.

Lyle accepted a cigarette and he it was who produced the lighter and touched the flame first to Barker's cigarette, then to his own. And again there was a certain ritualistic formality about this small and usually unimportant civility. A token guarantee, perhaps, that they were both, on the face of things, civilised men. Enemies, but at the same time friends. That this was a duel of wits and not a barbaric blood-letting based upon brute force.

They smoked in silence for a few moments then, as he leaned his head back, to blow smoke at the ceiling, Lyle murmured, 'Why did you run all the way home?'

'What?' Barker looked startled for the moment. As if the resumption of the questioning had caught him unawares. Or perhaps as if he'd been expecting another question to which he already had an answer. Startled and off balance.

'You ran all the way home.' Lyle still gazed at the ceiling.

'After I'd found the body?'

'Yes.' Lyle lowered his gaze to the file on the table. 'Why?'

'The – the shock.'

'But why run *home*?'

'To – to telephone. To . . .'

'You passed people.'

'Yes, I suppose I did. But . . .'

'Why not tell one of the people you passed?'

'I – I wanted the police. I . . .'

'You could have stayed by the body. Called for assistance.'

'It – it never entered my . . .'

'Why run home to telephone?'

'It seemed the quickest . . .'

'You passed two kiosks.'

'Oh!'

'Why all the way home?'

'I – I don't know. Shock, I . . .'

'You could have called from either one of two kiosks.'

'Yes. I – I know, but . . .'

'Dialled nine-nine-nine.'

'Can't you understand . . . ?'

'The quickest way, surely?'

'I know. Sitting here . . .'

'So why go all the way home?'

'I don't know.' A desperate quality entered Barker's tone. 'I just don't *know*.'

'When you arrived home . . .' Lyle slipped a typed quarto sheet from the file. '. . . you still didn't telephone.'

'No. I . . .'

'A statement from your wife. You ran upstairs.'

'When you saw her just now, did she . . . ?'

'The statement was taken some days ago. You ran into the house and upstairs. That's what she says.'

'Yes. I – I . . .'

'Why?'

'To the – to the bathroom.'

'Why?'

'Dammit, I wanted to vomit. To be sick. That's why . . .'

'From shock?'

'From seeing what I'd just...'

'How many suits have you, Mr Barker?'

'Wha-at?'

'Suits? Clothes?' Lyle smiled, patiently. 'How many suits?'

'Two. No...three.'

'Two? Or three?'

'Three. Two good ones. One rather old. But I don't see...'

'What colour?'

'What on earth...?'

'Your suits. What colour are they, Mr Barker?'

Lyle seemed to be concentrating most of his attention upon the typed quarto sheet. The smile was still on his lips. Still a patient smile; still a strangely long-suffering smile. Occasionally as he asked a question he glanced up, over the half-moons of his spectacles. But not always. Not at every question.

Barker said, 'They're blue. Navy blue.'

'All three?'

'Yes, all three. I don't see what you're getting...'

'What material?'

'Look, I can't see...'

'Blue serge? Like the one you're wearing?'

'Yes. Like – like the one I'm wearing, if you must...'

'And all your shirts are white, of course?'

'I don't see how you know...'

'Your wife mentioned it,' drawled Lyle.

'Oh!'

'And – presumably – all your shoes are black?'

Barker nodded.

Lyle was looking at the quarto sheet and didn't see the nod.

He looked up and said, 'Black?'

'Yes. Yes, they're all black.'

'Good. Good.' Lyle leaned back in his chair, thrust his left hand deep into his trouser pocket and with his right hand turned the half-smoked cigarette meditatively. He said, 'The picture then. You find the body. You're shocked . . . naturally. Still in a state of shock, you run home. You rush to the bathroom to vomit at what you've just seen. Then you return to the hall, telephone the police and arrange to meet them at – or near – the place where you found the body. Correct so far?'

'Yes. Yes, that's exactly what happened.'

Lyle stared at the glowing tip of the cigarette and said, 'Now . . . tell me what you were doing in the coppice.'

CHAPTER THIRTY

The rapport, followed by the gradual domination.

This, the very quintessence of a successful interview. The two personalities must first meet, must acknowledge each other, and become linked. Not merely two men: the policeman and the suspect; the interviewer and the interviewee. At that level it remains a simple question and answer session; a glorified quiz game. But an *interview* is far more than that.

Compress a marriage – the stresses, the strains, the give and the take of a prolonged marriage – into a time-span of a few hours and there you have, in effect, the ingredients of a successful (or an unsuccessful) interview. In the beginning there is a fusion of minds. On the face of things a mutual respect. Then over the years (over the hours) a dominant personality surfaces, is accepted and the marriage becomes complete . . . and the interview *becomes* an interview. There is no turning back. There is no 'fresh start'. The relationship is there and unalterable; there is an unspoken claim by one and a resigned acceptance by the other.

Many otherwise fine police officers remain confirmed 'bachelors' as far as the art of interviewing is concerned throughout their whole police career. They can ask questions, they can collect evidence, they can detect crime. But they can never *interview*.

Lyle could interview.

And he quietly stamped his domination upon Barker by means of that almost off-handed remark. 'Now . . . tell me what you were doing in the coppice.'

Barker caught his breath. His face lost a little of its

colour. He was like a man suddenly confronted with a near-impossible choice of evils; like a man in mild shock. He raised his cigarette to his mouth four, perhaps five, times. Jerkily. Sucking the smoke into his mouth, but not inhaling it. Then he squashed the cigarette into the tin ash-tray.

Lyle waited. He did not even look at Barker; he kept his eyes slightly out of focus, but trained at the darkening glow of the cigarette end. His domination had been established. It was enough. He was not a man to harry or badger his prey once the capture was complete.

Barker spoke. His voice was low. Harsh. From the back of a dry throat and forced out between dry lips.

He said, 'May I . . . ?' He tried to clear his throat, but the voice remained the same. He seemed to have lost the ability to manufacture spittle. He croaked, 'The – the toilet. May I please use the toilet?'

'Certainly.' Lyle moved his eyes from the cigarette end and smiled. 'Sergeant Adams will escort you. It's necessary, I'm afraid.'

'Oh!'

'People *have* been known to commit suicide . . .'

'No. I wouldn't do that.'

'Oh, I'm sure you wouldn't. But . . .' Lyle sighed. '. . . because of past incidents there are certain rules. Sergeant Adams will escort you. And he will, I'm afraid, insist that the door be left wide open.'

'Oh!'

'Precautions, you see.'

'Er – yes. I suppose . . . I suppose so.'

Adams wrote, '2.35 a.m. Barker requested to use toilet', then stood up from the chair by the door.

Lyle glanced at his wrist-watch and said, 'Shall we say twenty minutes, Mr Barker? No hurry. I think we're both in need of a break.'

126

CHAPTER THIRTY-ONE

Left alone in the all-purpose room Lyle once more washed his hands. The same near-eucharistical rite of soaping and sudding, of rinsing and symbolically purifying; of removing the skim of contamination and defilement which was part of the job. He also splashed cold water onto his face as a counter to bone-weariness which was a concomitant of the o'clock. A look of distaste touched his expression as he reached for the towel and saw the stain left by Barker as a result of Bell's assault.

Lyle shrugged his jacket back onto his shoulders, left the room, made his way along corridors, then left the police station by the rear door.

His intention had been a quiet stroll in the night air. A cleansing of the lungs after almost four hours of smoke-fugged atmosphere. The police station stood in its own grounds; a tarmac park at the rear for squad cars and officers' vehicles; neat lawns, bisected by concrete-slabbed paths, fringed with spaced rowan and plane trees down each side and, at the front, an imposing shrubbery, kept clean and clipped by the local Parks Department, on each side of the flight of shallow steps leading to the main entrance. Lyle had intended strolling from the rear to the front of the building – probably all the way round – as a respite from the strain of the interview.

So far he had caught Barker out in, perhaps, a dozen lies. Or, if not lies, half-truths. And so far he had not challenged Barker to explain those lies or half-truths. The ditch? The coppice? Yes, they were levers. Good levers, too. But in themselves they could be explained away. Two inconsistencies in a story didn't prove guilt; they could be excused – even justified – by any moderately clever defence. But upon those two could be built a massive, interwoven tapestry of untruths. Unnecessary untruths. Particularly unnecessary untruths when the questions from which they sprang concerned multiple rape and murder. But the tapestry had to be woven, and woven with all the skill at his command and, to do that weaving, he needed a clear mind.

He stepped out onto the tarmac and breathed in frost-nipped night air.

A voice said, 'Ah, Mr Lyle.'

In the temporary blindness resultant upon his leaving the well-lit police station, Lyle had not seen the chief inspector walking from his parked car and towards the rear door.

Lyle kept the annoyance from his voice as he said, 'Good morning, chief inspector.'

'Finished with Barker?' asked the C.I.

'No, sir.'

'Oh?' It was a questioning exclamation, carrying worry and vexation.

Lyle said, 'At the moment he's attending to the wants of nature. I thought a turn around the building – to stretch my legs a little – might not come amiss.'

'Somebody's with him, I hope.'

'Yes. Sergeant Adams.'

'Adams? Why not Bell?'

Lyle hesitated for a moment then committed himself. He said, 'Barker refused to be questioned with Bell present. He has no objection to Adams, apparently.'

'Does he have a choice?' asked the C.I., trenchantly.

'Bell?'

'No . . . Barker?'

'I *would* like him to answer some questions,' said Lyle, mildly.

'And what about the front office?' demanded the C.I.

'They know where Sergeant Adams is.' Lyle began his stroll. The chief inspector moved into step alongside him. Lyle added, 'Nothing's cropped up . . . obviously.'

'Nevertheless . . .'

'Barker's under formal arrest.' Lyle shoved his hands deep into his trouser pockets as he tossed this crumb of official comfort to the C.I. 'He's been cautioned. And, oh yes, his wife knows.'

'You're as sure as *that*?' The C.I. sounded less uneasy. 'That he's the murderer?'

'Yes.'

'He's the murderer,' drawled Lyle. 'We've certainly enough evidence to justify an arrest. And a prolonged interview. With a modicum of luck we should have enough evidence to charge him before morning.'

'Is that where Bell is?' asked the C.I.

'Bell?'

'Out seeking this evidence you need?'

'Oh, no.' Lyle smiled to himself in the darkness. 'Bell's gone off duty. There was nothing more he could do.'

'This evidence then? Where do you propose . . .'

'He'll make a statement.' There was no doubt at all in Lyle's tone. 'He's been on the point a couple of times. He'll make a full confession before we tuck him up for the night.'

'I think . . .' The C.I. stopped in mid-sentence.

'Yes?'

'It's one hell of a crime, Mr Lyle.'

'Triple murder. Triple rape,' agreed Lyle.

'I was thinking . . .' The C.I. hesitated again, then said, 'It might be wise to notify the superintendent. Possibly the Head of C.I.D.'

'In which case,' murmured Lyle, 'we all might as well go home to bed.'

'Oh!'

Lyle said, 'He'll talk to me. In the presence of Sergeant Adams. I can't guarantee he'll talk to anybody else. As a personal opinion I don't think he will.'

The chief inspector said, 'Oh!' again, then stopped and said, 'In that case I'd – er – I'd better get into the Charge Office. In case something's cropped up. They – er – they may need me.'

'It's possible,' agreed Lyle innocently.

'You'll – er – you'll keep me in the picture, of course?'

'Of course,' promised Lyle.

'Good. Good.' The chief inspector turned for the rear door of the building. 'I'll – er – leave Barker to you then. You and Sergeant Adams.'

'Yes, sir,' sighed Lyle and resumed his stroll.

Why, thought Lyle, *do they make them chief inspectors – acting divisional officers – before they've even learned their trade? Before they're even prepared to accept the responsibility?*

The man's frightened, and he has cause to be. In his shoes and with his limited experience I'd be frightened. But at least he has enough sense to be frightened. Thank the Lord for small mercies. With some young tearer-up-of-trees – with some men I could name – we'd be in real trouble.

Nevertheless...

Instinct, presumably. Not sense. Not past experience. But instinct tells him he's in for a roasting. Whichever way it goes. If Barker doesn't break, they'll have him for sanctioning the arrest and the interview. If he does *break, they'll damn soon let him know that they don't like being kept away from the kill. Chief inspectors – detective inspectors – don't handle multiple murder and multiple rape single-handed. Only gold braid steers a gold-braided enquiry.*

Such innocence!
He'll learn. He'll learn a little about me, too.
Me? I have my home. I have my independence. I'm within touching distance of retirement and I've reached the absolute limits of my promotion prospects. But I'd like a good one – this one – to crown the service.
I'd like to be able to . . .
'Inspector Lyle.'

The voice cut across his thoughts. It was a woman's voice, calling softly, from the shadows at the corner of the building. A frightened, timid voice; recognisable as a voice he had once heard, but not immediately identifiable as the voice of the outraged woman who, less than three hours before, had stormed into the Charge Office.

As she stepped from the shadow, she said, 'Thank God. I was hoping you might . . . That somebody might . . .'

She seemed unable to formulate whatever it was she wanted to say.

She was pale-faced and cold, unable to control the slight tremble which quivered her whole body as the night's nip drove its teeth bone deep. Her eyes were puffed and red-rimmed from weeping.

Lyle said, 'Mrs Barker. What on earth? I thought you'd gone home.'

'Half-way . . . then I turned back.'

'You've been waiting . . .'

'Yes.' She nodded and tried to smile, but failed.

'In heaven's name, why?'

'I don't know.' There was a strange, lost-child quality about her. All the certainty, all the self-confidence had gone and in its place there was something akin to heart-break. She whispered, 'I'm frightened, Inspector Lyle. Frightened!'

'Of going home alone? Of . . .'

'No.' The trembling increased and it seemed natural

and no more than humane that he place his arm across her shoulders to draw her fractionally closer for warmth and comfort. She muttered, 'Of tonight. Of the future. Of what I've done . . . and what I *might* have done.'

He guided her around the second corner, to the neon-lit main road and towards the police station's main entrance. But what solace could he give? What consolation when, within the time-span of minutes, he would be once more pitting will against will, wits against wits, with her husband, with a lifetime's imprisonment as a fit and proper forfeit?

He led her into the warmth of the police station, along the corridors and into the Interview Room; the same Interview Room in which they'd talked.

He said, 'Stay here. If anybody comes – asks – tell them you have my permission.'

'Thank you.' She lowered herself wearily onto one of the chairs.

'Cigarettes?' He tapped his pocket, then made the first movement to reach for his packet.

'No, thank you.' Once again she tried to smile. 'I have some. There was a machine. I got some. And matches.'

'Good.'

Lyle stood and watched her. Watched the tiredness drain the pride from her shoulders and the haughtiness from the hold of her head. Her present, outward appearance was one of complete submission to circumstances over which she had no control. Her wretchedness was far more than a mere physical thing; far deeper, far more basic, than a bodily weariness. It was a capitulation. Complete, absolute and without qualification.

Lyle tried to analyse his own feelings. He wanted to go, but at the same time he wanted to stay. One part of him was anxious – and more than anxious – to break Barker and force a confession from him. The other part of him shied away from the possibilities of what that confession might do to this woman; what self-torture it might trigger off in her.

She looked up at him and said, 'George . . .'

'He's having a break,' said Lyle gently, 'He – er – he needed a break. We both did.'

'Has he . . . ?' She left the question incomplete.

'Not yet.' Lyle forced himself to tell the truth because in the end the truth was very necessary. He said, 'He will . . . eventually.'

'Confess?'

Lyle nodded.

'You're sure? So very sure?'

Lyle said, 'Yes . . . I'm sure.'

'A solicitor . . .' she began.

'He's refused one. Just as he refused to see you.'

'Why?' There was soft desperation in her voice. 'Why won't he see me? Why won't he ask for a solicitor? Why won't he do *anything* to help himself?'

'I think . . .' Lyle chose his words deliberately and with great care. 'I think he has a conscience, Mrs Barker. I think he also has a monumental shame. The shame is something he must overcome. Something he *will* overcome. The conscience is the stronger of the two. That, to his credit.'

'And then?'

'Then . . .' Lyle's lips twisted into a sympathetic smile. '. . . it's up to a Crown Court jury. *Then* he'll need a solicitor. And a very good barrister.'

'You – you won't hurt him,' she pleaded.

'You have my word.'

'And – and . . . And if he *does* ask for me.'

'You'll be told, immediately.'

'Thank you,' she whispered. 'You've been very kind.'

Lyle closed the Interview Room door as he left.

CHAPTER THIRTY-TWO

Not too far removed from the medieval custom of giving the axe-man a gift prior to stretching your neck across the block. The fault is not his; the fault is that of the law; he, poor man, is only doing his job. The law demands a decapitation and, unfortunately, *he* happens to be the official decapitation expert. Pity him. Thank him. Give him a small token as proof of your understanding.

'Thank you. You've been very kind.'

Lyle still had his hands deep in the pockets of his trousers as he walked slowly along the corridor towards the all-purpose room. His thoughts were bitter, even self-condemnatory as he walked, head down, towards the final confrontation with Barker.

He was a good copper. A good detective. A *damn* good interviewer. He knew himself well enough to know that, neither immodesty nor false modesty blinded him to the simple truth. He had the knack and he'd perfected that knack until it was almost an art form. Give him a guilty man, give him time enough to talk and he'd strangle that guilty man with words.

Adams was standing at the wide-open door of the room and, as Lyle approached, Adams came to meet him. At a distance of little more than three yards from the door, they talked in subdued voices. They spoke in muttered tones and their words did not reach the ears of the waiting Barker.

Adams said, 'The toilet, sir. He wanted to be sick. That's all.'

'Oh!'

'Sick as a dog. He brought everything up. He's really scared.'

'Bell's assault, perhaps?' asked Lyle with a frown.

'No, sir.' Adams sounded quite positive. 'Fear, that's all.'

'Did he say anything?'

'No. Just puked his ring up. But he's bloody terrified.'

'We seem to have unsettled him, sergeant.'

'I'll say.'

'What we were after.' Then Lyle added, 'The chief inspector's back.'

'Oh, aye?'

'He knows where you are.'

'And – er – Bell?'

'Barker won't talk with Sergeant Bell present. That's why I sent Bell home.'

'So all we have to do now . . .' Adams grinned.

'That's all, sergeant. That's all we have to do.' Lyle sighed, then repeated, 'That's *all* we have to do.'

He walked into the all-purpose room. Adams followed, closed the door, then settled down on the chair to continue recording the interview. Lyle walked to his own chair, lowered himself into a sitting position and stared down the table at George Barker.

Barker looked ill. Genuinely ill. There was a deathly pallor about his face. The skin had an unhealthy sheen, a light film of perspiration, perhaps, but Lyle thought not. The eyes were at the same time wild but lustreless; like frightened animals, trapped and searching for an escape which was not there. The hands were finger-spread and palm-downwards on the surface of the table; as if pressing down on the polished surface for some sort of support.

Lyle's metamorphosis was complete within moments. From a slightly discomposed, even embittered, middle-aged man whose basic humanity was causing perverse feelings of culpability, to the immaculate interrogative machine, searching for an impossible, absolute truth. He was like a surgeon whose skill requires complete objectivity the moment he takes up the scalpel. Or, like a bomb-aimer, whose very sanity precludes him from an imagination which encompasses the innocent women and children he is about to destroy when he presses the release-button.

Lyle swung into action. His feelings were locked away behind thought-tight doors.

Adams wrote, '2.50 a.m. Interview resumes.'

CHAPTER THIRTY-THREE

Lyle settled the half-moon spectacles into place and said, 'You look unwell, Mr Barker.'

'No. It's – er . . . I'm quite all right.' The tips of Barker's fingers pressed fractionally harder against the surface of the table.

'Sergeant Adams tells me you've been vomiting. If you need a doctor . . .'

'No. No doctor . . . thank you.'

'Something you ate, perhaps?' smiled Lyle.

'No. I – I don't think so. I can't think of anything . . .'

'Or, guilt, perhaps?' The smile remained. A teasing smile. An intimidatory smile. Lyle added, 'Guilt plays havoc with the digestive system. We – by "we" I mean the working policeman – see it very often.'

Barker spoke through clenched teeth and said, 'I'm all right, inspector. As you say, it must have been something I ate. That, plus the fact that I'm not used to being questioned at this hour in a police station.'

'Quite.' Lyle bobbed his head as if in acknowledgement of the explanation and, as he moved the envelope-files nearer, said, 'We'll get back to the questioning, then. Get it over with as soon as possible.'

The tone did it; the comfortable, comforting tone; the warmth of mock-sincerity with which Lyle spoke. Like a man who, once hypnotised, can be readily re-hypnotised, so the rapport was immediately re-established. The con was complete within that short exchange and Barker visibly relaxed, his fingers eased their pressure on the table, some of the terror left his eyes, and he cleared his throat as if in preparation for an exchange of pleasantries.

'I think,' murmured Lyle, 'you can be accurately described as a man of habit. A man of routine. Would you agree?'

'I – er – I suppose so. I haven't given it much thought.'

'Consider it.' Lyle looked up from the files. 'Apart from the fixed routine of your employment, you rise and go to bed at about the same hour . . . that, at a guess. You take a stroll every evening, weather permitting, of course. You always wear the same sort of clothes, or so I'm told. Routine. Habit. Surely?'

'Yes.' Barker nodded slowly. 'Yes, I suppose I am. A person of habit.'

'Except at Southport,' said Lyle gently.

'Southport?'

'The evening stroll. You substituted an evening *drive*. I wonder why?'

'I wasn't at home. It was in a strange town. I didn't . . .'

'Nor were you at home in Bridlington. But in Bridlington you walked.'

'Oh!' Barker frowned, then his face cleared and he said, 'I remember . . . of course. I needed petrol. The tank was almost empty. I thought it wise to fill up that evening. I was starting for home the next day.'

'Such an *obvious* answer,' murmured Lyle.

'Yes. But . . .'

'But it's taken you months to remember it. Odd, wouldn't you say?'

'One doesn't remember such trivialities. Such little things are . . .'

'Mr Barker.' There was mild protest in the tone. 'There are no "trivialities" in a murder enquiry. A man of habit who breaks that habit, and he doesn't remember why until his fourth interview.'

'It was nothing. For heaven's sake what does a little thing like that prove?' Barker had regained composure enough to protest. Even to argue. He said, 'Who remembers when they buy petrol? Who remembers when . . . ?'

'*You* remember,' said Lyle mildly.

'Only because you've jogged my memory. Only because . . .'

'And the other interviews?'

'Nobody asked me.'

'The car . . . surely? You mentioned the car?'

'That I'd gone for a drive. That's all.'

'Ah, but you *didn't* "go for a drive", did you? You went to buy petrol.'

'Then I went for a drive. For a quiet drink.'

'Originally, though, to buy petrol,' pressed Lyle.

'Yes.' Barker nodded. 'Strictly speaking, yes. Then I decided to go for a drink.'

'At a public house in Birkdale,' intoned Lyle.

'Yes.'

'But you can't remember the name of the public house.'

'No. I'm sorry, I can't.'

'And you bought half a pint of beer.'

'Yes.'

'And took almost two hours to drink it.'

'Yes.'

'Leaving your car parked in a prohibited area.'

'Yes . . . so it seems.'

'Anything else?' asked Lyle pleasantly.

'I'm sorry, I don't quite . . .'

'That you might have forgotten?'

'No. I can't think of . . .'

'You'd forgotten the petrol, of course?'

'Yes. But . . .'

'Going to the dunes, for example?'

'What?'

'Going to the sandhills? With Pauline Standish?'

'For God's sake! I keep telling you ...'

'You do indeed,' said Lyle wearily. He sighed, then repeated, 'You do indeed. But unfortunately certain factors – more than that, certain facts – suggest that this, too, might be something you've "forgotten".'

'I can only say ...'

'One moment, Mr Barker, if you please.' Lyle raised a hand a few inches. His politeness was quite impeccable. His interruption was that of a civilised man quietly interrupting an interruption; claiming the right to bring his own argument to a logical conclusion. So punctilious, in fact, that it brought the ghost of an apologetic smile to the pale face of Barker. Lyle continued, 'Once, already, I've asked you to do this. Bear with me while I ask you again. Sit here in my chair, listen to a man say what you've been saying: that on a certain evening some few months ago he visited Southport . . . the same evening when a young girl was murdered. That on that same evening he visited Birkdale . . . the same evening the young girl was murdered *at* Birkdale. That this man claims to have visited a public house, but can't remember the name of that public house. That he ordered half a pint of beer and took two hours to drink it, but that nobody witnessed this uncommonly slow consumption. That he is a man of habit, but on this particular evening – the evening the young girl was murdered – he broke his habit . . . and, by breaking that habit, was on his own admission in Birkdale at the exact time of the crime. No alibi. No witnesses. And as far as we, the police, are concerned no other suspect. Sit in this chair, Mr Barker. Listen to what I've listened to. Then answer me. Would you not think it at least possible that this man murdered that young girl?'

The loaded question to end all loaded questions.

Framed in such a reasonable manner. Spoken with such simple appeal to common sense.

It demanded a reasonable answer. A common sense answer.

Barker nodded slowly then said, 'Yes. In your chair I would think it possible. Perhaps even more than possible.'

CHAPTER THIRTY-FOUR

And that, thought Adams, *just about stones the cherry. All we have to do now is chew. Then, when it's soft enough, swallow.*

Easy . . . when you know how.

Charlie Bell, old mate, you should be here at this moment. You should be learning. Muscle isn't in the same league. Lyle's pulled it without laying a glove on him. Lyle's smashed him – demolished him – ripped the rug from under him . . . and the poor, gormless idiot doesn't even know it's happened.

Check, thought Lyle. *Not yet checkmate, but certainly check.*

To admit, however indirectly, that you 'possibly' killed the Standish girl is all we need. From a 'possibility' to a 'probability', then from a 'probability' to a 'certainty'. That is the route you are about to take, my friend.

How long?

Who knows? Who cares?

You are tiring. Your wits are becoming dulled. Three hours ago you'd have evaded that trap. You wouldn't have made that admission.

Standish. Then Wallace. Then Roberts.

Then a statement . . . then to bed.

CHAPTER THIRTY-FIVE

The way of an interview – any interview – between a suspect and a police officer. The policeman starts by 'knowing'. Even without real proof, he 'knows' and, despite all pleas to the contrary on the part of the suspect, the policeman continues to 'know' throughout the first part of the interview. The colloquialisms covering this method of crime detection include 'bobbying by the seat of your pants', 'gut bobbying' and 'feeling it in your water'.

The interview progresses and, assuming the interviewee continues to claim his innocence (and assuming he *is* innocent), a gradual change takes place. Despite all this 'knowledge', 'gut bobbying' and the rest, a seed of doubt enters the policeman's mind and grows. Innocent men *have* been known to be charged and have even been known to be convicted and sentenced.

The previously firmly held 'knowledge' slips a little. The policeman, if he doesn't know his job, tends to panic and, in the end, the suspect takes over and dominates the interview. And the interview ends with the policeman having a face covered with egg.

But . . .

If the policeman knows his job that point of doubt can be successfully circumnavigated. It takes skill. It takes know-how. It also takes a small lifetime of experience. But it can be done.

The trick is to get the suspect to admit at least the *possibility* of his guilt. To con him. To carefully channel his answers until he is prepared to step aside from himself, make-believe that he is a third party and agree that, as this non-existent third party, he *might* be guilty.

Outside the confines of a police station – away from the false atmosphere of a prolonged interview – the situation is ludicrous; that a man might say, in effect, 'I didn't commit this crime, but it is possible that I did, I can understand how you might *think* I did.' The contradiction is ridiculous. It is a complete nonsense. He either did or he didn't. And if he didn't there is no 'possibility' that he did. To admit of that 'possibility' is tantamount to an admission of guilt.

And that is exactly what Lyle had achieved; an admission, albeit a very guarded admission, of guilt on the part of Barker.

Not even by the flicker of an eyelid did Lyle register this technical victory. He merely allowed a natural pause to edge its way into the interview, took cigarettes from his jacket pocket, chose one, then tossed the packet along the table towards the man he was about to break.

When they were both smoking – when, despite the pallor of his face, Barker was as composed as he'd been throughout the interview – Lyle continued the questioning. His voice was conversational; quietly discursive. Except for the place and the subject-matter they might have been two friends enjoying a pleasant tête-à-tête.

He said, 'The Bridlington problem. Shall we discuss that?'

'Yes ... of course.'

'Two months – thereabouts – after the Standish affair.'

'So I understand.'

'Now.' Lyle rolled ash from his cigarette into the ashtray. 'You were at this N.A.L.G.O. get-together. Not being a gregarious type you weren't interested in the drinking and chatting of the evening. You went for a walk . . . the old "habit" thing coming out again. Right so far?'

Barker nodded.

Lyle mused, 'A pleasant walk to Flamborough. To Flamborough Head and the lighthouse. A few lungfuls of clean, salt air then back to the hotel and bed. Still right?'

'That's what happened,' agreed Barker.

'You met nobody?'

'Nobody I knew. Nobody I can remember.'

'You can't remember passing Dane's Dyke?'

'I don't know where Dane's Dyke is. I might have passed it . . . I just don't know.'

'Will you take my word? That it's impossible to reach Flamborough Head, by land, without crossing Dane's Dyke? If necessary I'll get a large-scale map and show you.'

'I'll take your word,' said Barker.

'Good. Good.' Lyle inhaled cigarette smoke. 'It's dusk then. Almost dark. Solitude. To quote your own words – as I remember – you just "stood there". At the headland. Looking out to sea. Relaxing.

'The light flashing. Not a sound. No human voices. No gulls. Absolute quiet. Tranquillity would, I think, be an appropriate word to use.'

'It was very tranquil,' agreed Barker.

'And,' drawled Lyle, 'what sounds there might have been were, presumably, deadened by the sea mist. Is that the picture?'

'It was very nice,' said Barker.

'Ear-plugs?' asked Lyle innocently.

'What?' Barker frowned his perplexity.

'Were you wearing ear-plugs?' asked Lyle, still with a look of innocent curiosity on his face.

'Why on earth should I be . . . ?'

'I know Bridlington, old boy.' Lyle leaned back in his

chair, clasped his hands behind the back of his neck and gazed at a point about a yard above Barker's head. His voice remained low-pitched and reasonable, but with an underlay of mockery which belied any suggestion of genuine friendship. He said, 'Bridlington. Nice place. I know it well. I've spent a few holidays there. But – as you say – sea mists. Sea frets as they call 'em. They roll in, thick as the old-time pea-soupers sometimes. And those rocks off Flamborough Head. They have real teeth. To say nothing of the peculiarities of the tides.'

'I don't see what . . .'

'The old lighthouse,' mused Lyle refusing to be interrupted. 'Very beautiful at night, with the beam sweeping around like a searchlight. But not much good in fog. Visibility fifty yards . . . that's what you said, I think. And those rocks go well beyond fifty yards from the shore. Hence the foghorn.'

'Oh!'

'Quite.' Lyle interlinked his fingers, lowered his eyes until they stared straight into Barker's face and continued, 'Now, my friend, don't try another now-I-remember routine. I know that foghorn. At a fifty-yard visibility and anywhere near the base of the lighthouse station it *couldn't* be forgotten. It would be blasting your ears off. The one thing you *would* remember.'

Barker opened and closed his mouth twice, then for a third time, but seemed unable to speak.

'At the base of the lighthouse station,' repeated Lyle. 'At Bridlington you can just about hear it . . . if you listen for it. The same about half a mile inland . . . it points out to sea, that's why. The same at Dane's Dyke. You can hear it, but only if you're *listening* for it. If you're otherwise engaged . . .' He smiled, then purred, 'Busy. Raping and killing a seven-year-old child.'

'That's not true,' choked Barker and, suddenly, the

146

sheen on his chalk-white face grew into perspiration, which gathered and dripped from his chin.

'Listening to the surf,' mocked Lyle, gently. '*Hearing* the surf with a foghorn blasting your ears off.'

'I didn't kill her,' breathed Barker.

'Strolling along the cliff tops. Sea mist. Visibility fifty yards. But that stuff swirls a lot. Visibility nil at odd moments. Strolling along the cliff tops. Risking breaking your neck.'

'I didn't kill her.'

'Dusk. Near-darkness. Twenty minutes – thereabouts – you stood there, then you walked back. Still the sea mist. Along the cliff tops. No lights. Those cliff tops don't have street lighting, Barker. How did you do it? Radar?'

'I didn't kill her.'

Like a man clinging to a life-raft in a storm, Barker clung to those four words. He mouthed them – repeated them – until all meaning had been wrung dry and they were like dead sticks, threatening to crack and splinter beneath the sheer weight of his denial.

Lyle leaned forward slightly. His eyes narrowed; the forget-me-not blue had chipped ice floating on its surface. He removed the spectacles and when he spoke again his voice was as cold as his stare.

He said, 'Face the truth, man, for God's sake. You never went near Flamborough Head. You never went within a mile of the lighthouse. You've been feeding lies since you sat in that chair. Southport – and a girl dies in Birkdale. Bridlington – and a girl dies in Dane's Dyke. A "possibility" you said about Southport. Far more than a "possibility" when you harness it to Bridlington. Far more than a "possibility". Far more than a "probability". Lies upon lies upon lies. Tell me, Barker, when are we going to hear the truth? When are you going to stop taking me for a fool? When are you going to say something I might conceivably believe?'

'I didn't kill her. *I didn't kill her! I DIDN'T KILL HER!'*

The last time it was a scream. A shriek. The high-pitched howl of a trapped and mortally wounded animal.

His mouth remained open for a moment – gaping and with saliva sliming the lips – then he collapsed. The bones of his spine seemed to crumble and he fell forward, his face buried in arms folded across the table's surface, and he wept. Great hiccuping sobs which ripped through his frame and threatened to choke him.

Lyle watched him for a few seconds, then glanced at Adams and said, 'A glass of water, I think, sergeant, if you please.'

CHAPTER THIRTY-SIX

Inhumanity comes into it, too.

To watch a man suffer, as Barker was undoubtedly suffering, and to remain aloof from that suffering; to show stone-faced indifference to the agony inflicted, as the truth is torn from an unwilling suspect. This, too, is part of a successful, prolonged interview.

There is a saying, 'The better the bobby, the bigger the bastard', and there is much truth in that saying. Thus some men can never do it – they can never make themselves skilled interviewers – and nor is this to their discredit . . . as men. Their humanity is too great, they are incapable of standing back and viewing torment as a means to an end. They become involved. Their compassion is the genuine article and not a play-acted compassion (as with the expert interviewer) carefully controlled as one more weapon with which to attack the interviewee.

Ah, say the pundits, but think of the crime. Think of Barker's crime. Children. Not the so-called 'nymphets' of the hard-porn, under-the-counter magazines available at various 'sex shops'. Pay £5 – pay £10 – and, if your mind is so twisted, you may possess yourself of photographs of children of the age group of Standish, Wallace and Roberts, freely copulating with grown men. Pay £20 and animals, too, are included in the poses. But *these* children (Standish apart, perhaps) were not of the 'nymphet' fraternity. They were not being exploited and, as is so often the case, grinning their delight at this taste of adult perversion. Barker's victims had been just that . . . *victims.*

Victims of a crime calculated to make decent men and women sick to the stomach.

Therefore, say the pundits, think of the crime.

Away from the criminal, away from his agony immediately prior to his confession, it is easy. To concentrate upon the abomination and to have no pity for the man responsible for that abomination.

But . . .

Get to know him. Twist his very soul for hours on end. Pin him to a card, like an undead moth, and watch his wings flutter in their death throes. Then, if you are an ordinary man, realise that he, too, is deserving of pity. A differing pity than that reserved for his victims and a pity which is in no way transferred from them to him, but a pity nevertheless. A pity similar to that pity felt for a man with a warped and ugly body, but in this case a pity for a man with a warped and ugly mind . . . and who, himself, *knows* of its warp and ugliness.

A man like Barker, perhaps.

This if you are an ordinary man, but Lyle was no ordinary man.

Lyle felt no pity. No compassion. No sympathy. Lyle felt only disgust . . . and, be it understood, not disgust for the crimes and not disgust at the thought of the sufferings of the victims. His disgust was reserved for Barker; for Barker as a man who was less than a man. For this broken coward who wept when stronger men might have been angry. For Barker who hadn't even the guts to face the truth. For Barker the whimpering sub-human who was drowning in an ocean of self-pity.

Barker wept while, for a third time, Lyle went through the unnecessary formality of hand-washing. Barker wept while Lyle paced the floor of the multi-purpose room, impatient to have his opponent in a fit state to receive the *coup de grâce*.

But still Barker wept.

His weeping quietened, gradually, and only when Adams returned with a tumbler of water and, placing an arm across the sobbing man's shoulders, forced him to drink. Then slowly, painfully Barker regained control of himself.

Then Lyle sat down once more.

Adams returned to his chair by the door, placed the clip-board and foolscap on his knee, and wrote, '3.25 a.m. Resumption of interview.'

CHAPTER THIRTY-SEVEN

Lyle waited. He was now in complete control of the interview. The rapport was still there, but it was a different
type of rapport; a rapport similar to that which exists
between trainer and performing animal; a rapport built
upon domination and the acceptance of domination.
However long the interview now, Lyle had already won.
He need only wait for his victory. He could make Barker
jump through any hoop he chose, make him perform any
trick he felt justified in making him perform. Like lord
and vassal – like master and slave – that was the only
rapport left.

Therefore Lyle waited.

Barker sniffed a few times, took out a handkerchief,
wiped his eyes, blew his nose then, as he returned the
handkerchief to its pocket, said, 'I'm sorry, inspector. It
won't happen again. I'm very sorry.'

'That's quite all right.' Lyle's tone was still friendly, but
with a hint of airy understanding. 'Men crack under
interrogation. You're not the first. You won't be the last.'

'Nevertheless . . .'

'If you feel fit enough to continue.'

'Yes. Yes, I'm quite all right now. Please – y'know – go
ahead. Ask your questions.'

'The obvious question, then.' Lyle rested his elbows on
the surface of the table, linked his hands and steepled his
forefingers. 'Why lie about Bridlington?'

'I didn't . . .' Barker took a deep breath, then said, 'I
didn't actually *lie*. Not . . . *lie*.'

'Oh come, now,' sighed Lyle. 'Don't let's have to start
at the beginning again. No more of that ridiculous fairy

tale about standing on the headland listening to the waves wash upon the beach. There isn't a beach at Flamborough Head, Barker. And if there *was* you certainly couldn't have heard the waves above the sound of the foghorn. Those are facts. And those facts make you a liar. The truth . . . if you don't mind.'

Lyle rested the tips of his steepled forefingers against his lips. It was a prim gesture, the gesture of a sardonic housemaster awaiting the empty excuses of some misbehaved schoolboy.

Nor did Barker look too much unlike an elderly, caught-out schoolboy facing a mildly outraged housemaster. His hair was untidy. His tie was askew. His face was pale and still carried the run-marks of his tears.

He reached across the table and picked up his packet of cigarettes. He opened the packet, made as if to offer Lyle a cigarette then, realising that only one cigarette remained in the packet, forced a quick, apologetic smile from his lips and lit the cigarette with his own throw-away lighter.

Lyle waited with Buddha-like patience.

Barker began to talk. At first in quick, half-formed sentences, punctuated with quick inhalations from the cigarette. Then as he was allowed to continue uninterrupted his confidence increased; the sentences became less rambling and more complete.

He said, 'The – er – the Bridlington . . . The N.A.L.G.O. conference. It – it wasn't . . . What I mean is . . . it wasn't quite that way. Not – not what I've said. Well . . . not *exactly* what I've said.

'The conference . . . That's true. Of course it's true. And I don't like drinking sessions. Even – even mild drinking sessions. I – er – I hope I haven't given the impression of an orgy. Anything like that. Just that the delegates get together round the bar. And talk. And tell stories. That sort of thing. But – but that's something I can't do. I'm not that kind of a man. I can't "join in".

'And – my marriage. I've told you about my marriage. It's – it's that. That's part of it. Edwina. And the way she . . . I have my – my wants. My needs. I'm normal in that respect. I'm not a pervert. I'm not yet an old man. I need . . . certain things. Sex.'

He seemed to gather himself, to steady himself before the final race for a finishing-line which was a new truth. A truth – if it was the truth – of which he was ashamed and yet, at this particular moment of self-preservation, unashamed. He drew deeply on the cigarette then continued.

'Sometimes. When I'm away from home. Often in fact. I go with women. That's where I was. With a woman.'

'With a whore?' murmured Lyle, his finger-tips still touching his lips.

'Yes. A whore. You could call them that, I suppose.'

'What else?'

'Er – prostitutes. That's what they are, I suppose.'

'What else?' repeated Lyle flatly.

'Well, that's – that's it, you see. I was with this – this prostitute. I didn't go to Flamborough. Nowhere near Flamborough. I was with this woman.'

'Which woman?'

'This prostitute . . . when I said I was at Flamborough. And at Southport, too. At Birkdale. I – I didn't go for a drink. I was with this woman.'

'Same woman?' asked Lyle idly.

'Eh?'

'You keep using the words "this woman". As if there's only one. As if she meets you. At Bridlington. At South-port. A mistress of some sort who . . .'

'Oh, no! Different ones. Not the same one. A different one each time.'

'Interesting,' smiled Lyle.

'I'm – er – sorry.' Barker frowned. 'I don't see . . .'

'No more half-pints of beer. No more lighthouses. Now it's ladies of the street. Slags . . . to use the somewhat crude terminology.'

'Look, a man doesn't like . . .'

'*You* obviously do.'

'It's – it's my wife. She . . .'

'Was your wife with you, then?' The question was asked with just the right amount of mock-seriousness.

'For God's sake! Of course not. That's not what . . .'

'Then why bring *her* into it?'

'It's her fault,' said Barker desperately. 'She's the one to blame. Fundamentally.'

'Not you?'

'No. Not really. She's . . .'

'You're not the one who sought the company of some prostitute?'

'Yes. Of course I did. But . . .'

'You always,' said Lyle, softly, 'have the ready answer. The glib excuse. Home-spun psychology. All the sub-conscious reasons – for everything – reduced to simple language and available in cheap magazines on any book-stall. These days nobody does anything because he *wants* to do it. You go to bed with a couple of tarts, or so you say, but not because you have lustful desires. Oh, no. That would be too easy. Untie all the knots. Make every two-plus-two add up to a neat half-dozen. And it's not your fault at all. It's your wife's fault. Which makes every-thing okay. You weren't tempted. You didn't fall. You were pushed. I'm sorry, Barker, it's a line of argument I don't buy.'

'It's – it's an alibi,' said Barker vehemently. 'It proves I wasn't – I didn't . . .'

'Their names, please?' drawled Lyle.

'Who?'

'The two whores. The one at Southport. The one at Bridlington. Their names and their addresses, if you don't mind.'

'I – I – I don't know.'

'You called them *something* . . . surely?'

'N-no.'

'Nice. Nice.' Lyle tapped his lips, gently, with the tips of his steepled forefingers. 'The mind boggles. Non-identifiable fornication. Copulation on a "Hey you" basis.'

'I – I never asked,' stumbled Barker.

'You propositioned them . . . surely?'

'Well – er – no . . . not exactly.'

'You interest me, Barker.' The mild sarcasm was pure 'schoolmaster'. The subject-matter was triple murder, triple child-rape, but Lyle's slightly raised eyebrows and gentle curl of lips belonged to the classroom; to the not-too-popular master enjoying himself at the expense of a non-attentive pupil. He drawled, 'The – er – manner of approach at such moments. Presumably somebody makes the first move in these matters. An initial opening gambit. I've often wondered. Tell me. As an expert . . . explain things, please.'

'I'm – I'm not an expert,' muttered Barker.

'But obviously you know how.'

'I – I use taxi drivers.' Barker fought to answer a question which he knew was a goad; he fought to answer it as if it was a legitimate and reasonable enquiry. 'I . . . I g-go to the rank. The taxi rank, I mean. And – and then I get into conversation. With the drivers. I – I tell them what I want. That I'm looking for a – a woman. A prostitute. And – and they seem to know. One of them always knows. S-somebody.'

'And?'

'W-well, that's it. He drives me to the – to the address.

156

I don't know the address, I never ask. Then – then he goes to the door. D-does the arranging. Then – then I pay him. Give him something extra for – er – for *knowing*. And ask him to call back for me in two hours. That's – that's how it's done. How *I* do it.'

'Good lord!' Lyle's pretended surprise was an open mockery.

'That's – that's what happened,' said Barker. 'At Bridlington. And at Southport ... at Birkdale. That's what *really* happened.'

'But you don't know the names of these – er – ladies?'

'No, sir.'

'Nor where they live. Their exact address?'

'Er – no, sir.'

'The name of any of the taxi drivers?'

'No. There was no need for me to ...'

'The registration numbers of their vehicles?'

'No, sir.' Barker heaved a sigh of defeat, squashed what was left of his cigarette into the ash-tray, and said, 'No, sir. I don't know any of the names. Or the addresses. Or the numbers of the taxi cabs. But – but can't you see? It's – it's the truth. It's something I daren't tell you before. I was too ashamed. I was ... I was ... My God, it's the truth! Can't you *see* that?'

Lyle unsteepled his forefingers, but kept his hands linked. He lowered his hands until the palms and the inside of his forearms were flat on the table's surface. He leaned forward and peered over the half-moons of his spectacles as he spoke.

'What do I see?' he said. 'I see three children sexually assaulted then murdered. That is what I see, Barker. That is all I see and all I am allowed to see. Indeed, all I *want* to see. I am, however, aware of certain facts and those facts are related to what the criminal law tabulates as "means", "motive" and "opportunity".

157

'Those facts tell me that you were in the vicinity of the three crimes under investigation; in the vicinity of each crime on the day that crime was committed, and at the time when that crime was committed. Each time near enough to the scene of the crime to have committed that crime. I am aware, therefore, of your opportunity. You also had the means. Strangulation. You have hands. The victims were all children. Each child was manually strangled. You have, therefore, the means. The motive? Well now, the sexual assault in each case is motive enough for the murder. Self-preservation. The assurance that your petty "respectability" remains untarnished. Motive for the sexual assaults? Motive for child-rape?' His eyes hardened and his voice altered. 'Shall we call it "Cindy"? I know all about Cindy, Barker. I am aware of the flaw in your make-up. I know *what* happened – exactly what happened – and *when* it happened. If necessary I can bring proof and I'm prepared to wager that that proof would be allowed in court – as evidence of your peculiarities. Men like you don't change, Barker. I speak from much experience. They hold themselves in check for so long – for just so long – then the madness touches them once more . . . and a "Cindy" situation suddenly presents itself. They lose control. And that periodic loss of control is all the "motive" needed. You have a problem, Barker. A very serious problem. And you haven't solved that problem by substituting one set of lies for another.

'Why should I reject a lie about a walk along the cliff tops – a lie about a lighthouse – and then accept a lie about an unknown trollop? Why should I dismiss a lie about a nameless public house and then believe a lie about a nameless address?

'I'll tell you what *I* think, Barker. What *my* opinion is. Your infernal "respectability" . . . that's at the bottom of it all. The thing you value more than anything else on

God's earth. But you're in trouble. You're in very serious trouble. The chances are you'll be convicted of three particularly foul crimes. Of being sent to prison for a very long time. Something must be sacrificed . . . and you're prepared to sacrifice the thing you hold most dear. Your precious "respectability". Anything to stay free. You're even prepared to accept the tag of whoremonger. That's how desperate you are, Barker. A silly argument. A silly gamble. Placing such value upon this "respectability" . . . which you don't even possess.'

There was the soft sound of Adams's ballpoint on paper as he recorded the last of Lyle's words. Such was the depth of the silence; so absolute was the absence of any other sound. The room – this all-purpose room – seemed to have developed a faint echo. An echo so faint that it seemed to accentuate the silence and, like a series of 'everlasting mirrors', Lyle's accusation seemed to continue until it tapered off into infinity.

Lyle and Barker sat motionless facing each other. The silence of defeat gazing at the silence of victory.

Then Barker breathed, 'Cindy . . .' and left the name hanging in the silence like a self-condemnation.

'Your wife, too, knows how to hate,' said Lyle quietly.

There was another thirty seconds or so of silence. Utter silence. Not one of the three men in the room moved. Even their breathing seemed to be quietened; as if the absence of sound was a sacred thing and not to be defiled. Then when Barker spoke it was softly, gently, and as from a great distance. Nor did he seem to be speaking to Lyle. Rather did he seem to be mouthing a very personal – very private – creed; a doctrine of which he was the high priest; a faith, long secret from the outside world.

He said, 'Inspector, the meek may, indeed, inherit the earth. But not the weak. The weak inherit only one thing. The contempt of mankind. They know the difference between solitude and loneliness. They are the most lonely people in the world. They are unloved and they are incapable of commanding respect. Cindy . . .' He glanced over his shoulder, towards Adams, and said, 'You have no need to record this, sergeant. It has no bearing upon the murder of the three children.' Adams appeared not to hear. He continued writing as Barker went on, 'Edwina, my wife, knows how to hate, inspector. We agree upon that point. She presumably told you about Cindy. Did she tell you that I also love Cindy? That Christmas – so long ago – the evil found its way into my brain? She's a very honest woman. She won't have exaggerated. But certain things she doesn't know. And doesn't want to know. And never will know. That I, too, have suffered. God, how I've suffered. This hand . . .' He lifted his right hand a few inches from the table. 'To right that wrong I would happily take an axe and chop it off. Not for sympathy, inspector. I don't expect sympathy. I don't deserve sympathy. I would maim myself – willingly – just to be allowed to have a niece, whom I love, not to be everlastingly warned against "Uncle George".

'Tonight. Since I arrived here. You think you've frightened me. You think you've broken me perhaps. Inspector Lyle, I was a broken man before I arrived. Long before I arrived. Ask me the questions. I'll give the answers you want. Any answers. Tell me what answers you require . . . I'll give them. What I had when I arrived here – the one thing I had left and the one thing I clung onto – dignity. A weak man's dignity. By your yardstick – by Edwina's yardstick – a dignity I had no right to claim. And yet . . . a dignity. The dignity which comes only with continual humiliation. With a pain which is not a bodily pain. *My* dignity. You've stripped me of even that. I've nothing left. Ask your questions. Tell me what you want me to say. I'll say it . . . then let me rest.'

CHAPTER THIRTY-EIGHT

Gently, gently, thought Lyle. *This man requires a very special technique. This man won't easily break. He has grown so used to mortification it has become part of his personality. Self-abasement is his strongest weapon . . . but he hasn't the sense to realise it.*

Or has he?

Must I credit him with a guile he doesn't possess?

Will he bend, rather than break? Will he yield, rather than snap? Is his shame a clever sham? Or is he truly brow-beaten? Genuinely humbled?

No!

No man can crawl like this as a deceit. It has to be true. He must *be the disgusting, spineless nobody he claims to be.*

Therefore . . .

Gently, gently, Lyle. Play it as it comes. You still have all the trump cards. Play them carefully. He won't bend . . . he'll break!

CHAPTER THIRTY-NINE

'A long session,' observed Lyle, as he pushed himself upright from the chair. He glanced at his wrist-watch. It showed 4.20 a.m. He stretched his arms, smothered a yawn, then said, 'I think it's time we talked about Gwendolen Roberts . . . if you don't mind.'

Barker moved his shoulders resignedly.

Lyle placed his spectacles on the table alongside the trio of envelope-files. He shoved his left hand into the pocket of his trousers and, as he talked, he paced the room.

His walk was slow-paced and deliberate; a steady, stiff-legged, heel-to-toe perambulation. His head was sunk deep onto his chest, as if weighed down with the burden of hewing a seam of truth from a mountain of dross. His right hand was never still, rarely rising above waist-height, but moving restlessly in determinate gestures; emphasising, dismissing, taking each fact – each tiny admission – and placing it carefully into a growing store of damning evidence.

'A nice evening,' he said musingly. 'Thursday the third. A nice evening after a rather miserable day. Just the sort of evening to take a dog for a walk . . . right?'

'Yes, sir,' murmured Barker.

'On the common,' continued Lyle. 'A bit wet underfoot. The grass a bit damp but, if you're well-shod, a nice evening. Wet leaves, though. In the ditch, I mean, wet leaves in the ditch.'

He paused and Barker once more said, 'Yes, sir.'

'You have your suits dry-cleaned so I'm told?'

The question was so unexpected – so out of context – that Barker caught his breath before he said, 'Yes, sir. I like to look smart.'

'Often?'

'Yes.'

'Regularly?'

'Yes, sir.'

'How regularly?'

'Every fortnight. Every alternate Friday.'

'Good. Good.' Lyle walked four silent paces, then said, 'The question you didn't get round to answering, Barker. Just, exactly, what were you doing in the coppice?'

'The – er . . . the coppice?'

'We established . . . remember? When you found the body. Roberts's body. It was in the ditch. You had to *be* in the ditch to spot it. Remember? Crossing the ditch. That's what you said. Coming from the coppice. What were you doing in the coppice?'

Barker did not give an immediate answer. One of his hands strayed towards the packet of cigarettes on the surface of the table, then he remembered it was empty. As he passed the table Lyle slipped a hand into a pocket of his jacket, then dropped a packet of cigarettes onto the table within reach of Barker's hand.

Barker muttered, 'Thanks.'

'The coppice?' repeated Lyle.

'Well – you see – I have . . .' Barker chose and lit a cigarette as he answered the question. The tiny formality provided natural pauses in his reply; pauses in which he could, perhaps, elect a choice of words or settle upon a specific phrase. He said, 'I have a hobby, you see. It's . . . ornithology. Bird-watching. I take . . . I take every opportunity possible. Most evenings, in fact. When I go for my walk. I keep my eyes open for . . . for unusual birds.'

'You had your binoculars with you?' asked Lyle mildly.

'Oh, yes. You can't really pursue the hobby without...'

'In the coppice?'

'Yes. That's where I was. What I was doing.'

'And the dog?'

'What?'

'Spot, the dog. Was he in the coppice with you?'

'No. Oh, no. You can't do with a dog racing around when you're...'

'When you're enjoying the peepshow.' Lyle ended the sentence for him.

'I – er – I beg your pardon?'

'The peepshow. Courting couples. Your wife calls it voyeurism ... we call it "pimping". A wrong use of the word, I know. But that's what we call it. Pimping.'

'Inspector, if you seriously think...'

'Yes, I "seriously think", Barker. Your wife's seen you at it at least a couple of times. She's caught you at the bedroom window a few times, too. And a couple of years ago – thereabouts – you came home with a bloody nose. Binoculars come in useful for that particular – er – hobby. So do coppices. Uncontrolled dogs, on the other hand, tend to give the game away.'

Barker smoked the cigarette and remained silent.

'Bird-watching?' mocked Lyle gently.

'You seem to know a lot about me,' said Barker slowly.

Lyle smiled and made no comment. He continued his steady prowl and waited for Barker's next remark.

Barker muttered, 'It – it does no harm.'

'Pimping?'

'I'm not the only one, inspector.'

'Agreed.'

'And I've already explained about...'

'But – as far as you know – you were the only one in that coppice on the evening of the murder.'

'I can't see how...'

'And the murder was committed in the coppice.'

'That's taking a lot for granted. That's . . .'

'That's taking *nothing* for granted, Barker. You were in the coppice. The Roberts girl was assaulted, then killed, in the coppice. And the times tally. Tell me. What am I taking for granted?'

'That I killed her,' breathed Barker.

'Did you?' It was an academic question asked in a gentle, scholarly voice.

'Of course I didn't.'

'The "of course" prefix doesn't follow.'

'All right, I didn't. Does that satisfy you?'

'As a denial. But not, necessarily, as the truth.'

'How do you know,' asked Barker, hoarsely, 'that I was the only one in the coppice that evening?'

'Weren't you?'

'I don't know. I don't claim to know. I don't . . .'

'In which case I could turn the question inside out. How do you know you *weren't* the only person in the coppice?'

'I've already said. I don't know.'

'Roberts was there.'

'Obviously.'

'So was her murderer.'

'Obviously.'

'And *if* you were the only other person there . . . what then?'

'I can't have been. Can I?'

'But, my dear Barker, you've already said. You don't *know* whether any other person was in the coppice – other than yourself and Roberts, that is.'

To twist an argument. To take a logic and make it illogical. To turn an apparent fact 'for' and, by choice of words, transform it into an apparent fact 'against'.

These are the skills of the expert interrogator. Not to

shout, not to bluster and, wherever possible, not even to contradict. To prove the victim wrong by use of the victim's own words, to allow him to blunder from trap to trap, to use words as a binding-wire until he is unable to move. No so-called 'truth drug' is needed. No rack or thumbscrew. Pain – simple, uncomplicated physical pain – is a clumsy instrument by comparison.

Looked at objectively the skills of interrogation are simple enough. To ask the same question a thousand times in a thousand different guises, and at a thousand unexpected moments. That's all. To recognise a lie, but to keep that lie hidden – to accept it as the truth until its exposure is as wounding as a sword-thrust. To give a man, even a man like Barker, a feeling of security; to discuss rather than question and, via this discussion, create what on the face of it is a once-in-a-lifetime homogeneity.

To do all this . . . but slowly. Oh, so slowly.

The distance from a denial to a confession is a long and tiring journey. It is no quick, nip-round-the-corner thing. It is an Everest of talk; a light-year of words; a star-trek of apparent inconsequentialities. And, as the journey progresses – as the passage of time becomes measured by hours and sometimes even days – the strength and staying-power of the interrogator must surpass that of the interrogatee.

The friendship that is not a friendship. The verbal intercourse which has naked blades beneath its surface. The dialogue which is spiced with poison.

That is an interrogation. That is an interview.

And there comes a point where the interviewer, if he knows his art, can see the finish line ahead. When he knows that one final burst will allow him to breast the tape ahead of his victim.

Lyle had that knowledge and, within himself, he allowed himself the luxury of a smile.

He said, 'Gwendolen Roberts was raped and strangled in the coppice.'

'I know,' mumbled Barker.

'You *know*?'

'Because I've been told.'

'Ah, yes, because you've been told.'

'For God's sake! You don't think...'

'I don't know,' said Lyle mildly. 'Only *you* know that.'

'Do you seriously think...?'

'Somebody did.' Lyle's voice was less mild. 'Somebody killed her. Somebody dragged her body to the ditch and made an effort to hide it. *Somebody* did.'

'I keep telling you. I *found* her in the ditch.'

'You keep telling me,' agreed Lyle. 'That you found her. That you recognised her.'

'Yes.'

'Face downwards.'

'Her clothes. I recognised her...'

'School uniform.' Lyle continued his slow, stiff-legged pacing. 'You recognised her school uniform.'

'Yes.' Barker nodded.

'Don't be a damn fool!' For the first time Lyle put bite into his tone. 'A school uniform. Filthy. Torn. Blood-stained. And the wearer is face downwards in a ditch. Half-covered in muck and leaves. Wearing what? A uniform worn by hundreds of other kids. And you "recognised" her. Without even touching her.'

'I – I didn't touch her.'

'But you recognised her... so you claim?'

'Yes,' breathed Barker.

'How?' Lyle stopped alongside the table, looked down at Barker, and said, 'Exactly *how* did you recognise her? Not by her school uniform... I'll not wear that. Not by her hair – not by the back of her head... I'll not wear that either. Unless you personally dumped her there, how

167

in God's name did you recognise her as Gwendolen Roberts?'

'No . . . No . . . No . . .'

The single tiny negative. The one puny, panted denial. The impression was that Barker was allowing the last of his resistance to drip from his system. That soon he'd be drained. That he had not merely lost the will to fight, he'd just about lost the will to live.

Lyle moved to the end of the table. He threaded the tubular-steel and canvas chair between his legs, leaned his forearms along the back of the chair and, resting his chin on his arms, stared the length of the table at Barker's drawn and pallid face.

The tape was there. The finishing line was in sight. Lyle steadied himself – took a few deep breaths – then hared for the prize.

CHAPTER FORTY

The problem of describing that last sprint is the problem of words. The inadequacy of words. The imperfection of mere words in their description of the spoken word. To say that a remark is simple, gentle, soft, mild or, indeed, any one of a hundred different degrees of courteousness and moderation, is to do no more than hint at the truth. In the same way to describe an answer as frightened, or breathless, stammered or terrified, is to suggest harsh colours when the whole exchange was washed in varying pastel hues.

It was a gavotte, rather than a swing session; a Gregorian chant, rather than a Mahler symphony.

But the cigarette-smoking episodes were a thing of the past. Neither man sought imagined courage or mock calm through the inhalation of tobacco smoke. They sat facing each other. Little more than two yards apart. And they were still, with the stillness of a threatened whirlwind. Only their eyes and their mouths moved as they played this final round of verbal poker, whose prize was guilt or freedom.

Lyle said, 'You found her?'

'Yes.'

'There in the ditch?'

'Yes.'

'Bloody? Murdered? Ravished? Covered in filth? Half-hidden by leaves? Face downwards?'

'Yes'

'But you recognised her?'

'Yes. I recognised her.'

'As Gwendolen Roberts?'

'Yes.'

'No doubts? You knew it was her?'

'Yes. I knew it was her.'

'You ran home?'

'Yes . . . naturally.'

'Past two telephone kiosks?'

'It – it would seem so.'

'You know the district?'

'Yes.'

'You know the route you took?'

'Of course.'

'Does it not pass two telephone kiosks?'

'Yes . . . it passes two telephone kiosks.'

'Neither of which were vandalised.'

'I don't know. That's something I don't know.'

'Will you take my word for it?'

'Of course.'

'You could have telephoned from either one of those kiosks?'

'I – er – I suppose so.'

'*Couldn't* you?'

'Yes . . . had I thought.'

'What does that mean?'

'I was panic-stricken. I'd just found a murdered child. I wasn't thinking clearly.'

'When you arrived home you didn't call the police? Not immediately?'

'Not immediately.'

'Why?'

'I've already told you . . .'

'Tell me again.'

'I was ill.'

'Ill?'

'Sick. I wanted to vomit.'

'You didn't vomit at the scene.'

'No. No, I – I didn't vomit at the scene.'

'Why not?'

'I – I don't know. One doesn't control these things. They just happen.'

'But you were sick when you arrived home?'

'Yes. Violently sick.'

'The bathroom, I think?'

'Yes, the bathroom.'

'Your wife didn't see you?'

'No.'

'Hear you come into the house, perhaps?'

'Perhaps. I don't know.'

'Amplify that statement, please.'

'She doesn't care. Neither of us cares. We live under the same roof . . . that's all.'

'But she knew it was you?'

'I suppose she guessed.'

'And when you were in the bathroom ill?'

'She doesn't care. Believe me, Lyle, she doesn't *care*.'

'You were sick?'

'Yes.'

'Then you returned to the hall and telephoned the police?'

'Yes.'

'And arranged to meet them at the scene?'

'They asked. There was no point of reference. They asked me to go back and meet them there.'

'And you agreed?'

'Yes. Naturally.'

'Earlier this evening – yesterday evening – I showed you a photograph.'

'Yes.'

'You didn't want to look. Remember?'

'Yes, I remember.'

'I asked you a question.'

'Did you? I can't...'

'A specific question. "Is that how you left her?" Remember the question?'

'I – I think so.'

'You agreed. That's how you "left her".'

'I don't know what...'

'A question likely to be asked of a murderer.'

'For God's sake!'

'You accepted it. The question. You accepted it.'

'It *was* how I left her. How the police found her when...'

'Nevertheless, a question likely to be asked of a murderer.'

'You're twisting my words. You're...'

'You agreed. It was the sort of agreement a murderer might make.'

'What you're saying... It's – it's...'

'If you killed Roberts, you killed Standish and Wallace.'

'But I never... I haven't...'

'Carbon copies, Barker. Perfect replicas. One man, three murders.'

'I – I didn't kill Roberts.'

'Standish?'

'No.'

'Wallace?'

'No! How many more times? I was...'

'I know. You were with a woman ... or you were gazing out to sea. You were with a woman ... or you were enjoying a quiet drink. Anything, but killing children.'

'Look, if I lied, it was because...'

'You lied. You're still lying.'

'You've no right ... You've no proof...'

'You reported the murder of Roberts?'

'Of course. I can't see what...'

'Having passed two kiosks? Having visited the bath-room in order to vomit?'

'Do we have to go through all that ... ?'

'You reported the murder to the police and met them at the scene?'

'Yes.'

'Co-operated with the police as much as possible?'

'Of course.'

'Statements, for example?'

'Yes. Three statements. One about each murder.'

'Statements containing lies?'

'I ... Look, it's not that I ...'

'Statements containing lies?'

'Yes. All right. At least, not *all* the truth.'

'At the Roberts killing you handed in your clothes?'

'Yes. For forensic ...'

'Normal procedure. Clothes. Shoes. For forensic ex-amination.'

'Yes.'

Lyle flicked his eyes at the salmon-pink envelope-files.

He said, 'It's in there. The report from the forensic science lab.'

'I – I expect it is.'

'They're very thorough.'

'Who?'

'The forensic scientists. Very thorough. They examine every inch microscopically.'

'I – I suppose they do.'

'No mention of leaves. No mention of leaf-mould. No mention of muck from the ditch. No mention of traces of vomit.'

'Oh!'

'Just what might be expected. Traces of grass from the common. Rabbit droppings. That sort of thing.'

'Oh!'

'You changed clothes, Barker. When you arrived home you changed clothes before you telephoned the police.'

'I – I...'

'Identical suit. Identical shirt. Identical shoes. So easy. You changed clothes.'

Barker didn't answer.

Lyle said, 'You'd been in the coppice. Nobody must know you'd been in the coppice. That's where Gwen Roberts was murdered.'

Barker still didn't answer.

Lyle said, 'Blood, too. Semen. Probably vomit . . . that, too. But you *had* to change clothes before you called the police.'

'I – I touched her.'

'Touched her?'

'To – to see her face. To be *sure*. There was – there was blood . . .'

'You're finished, Barker. Your luck's run out.'

'I – I – I . . .'

'Thursday. Dry-cleaning every other Friday. The murder one day, clean clothes the next.'

'It – it – it's not like that. It's just that – just that . . .'

'Just that what?'

'I'm – I'm sorry.'

'Of course.'

'Truly sorry.'

'Naturally.'

'I seem to be . . . Seem to be . . .'

'What?'

'There's no way out . . . is there?'

'You've lied too much, Barker. A lot too much.'

'Such a lot. So many lies.'

'No more though . . . eh?'

'No. No more lies, inspector. I'll – I'll say what you want me to say.'

'The truth? Just for a change?'

'I – I can't fight any more. I'm tired. I'm beaten.'

'You killed Roberts?'

'Yes.'

'After sexually assaulting her?'

'Yes.'

'And Standish?'

'Yes.'

'And Wallace?'

'Yes.'

'All three?'

'Yes.'

'Sexual assault . . . then murder?'

'*Yes. Yes. YES!*'

CHAPTER FORTY-ONE

Played a certain way a violin string is capable of cracking a wineglass. That final 'Yes' could, or so it seemed, have shattered a glass factory. It bounced and ricocheted from wall to wall, from ceiling to floor; it hung, suspended and quivering in the air; it seemed to be imprisoned within the room. Tortured. Tormented. And again, or so it seemed, most unwilling to die.

Then there was silence.

Barker rested his elbows on the surface of the table, then lowered his head and clasped his ears and temples, as if that final affirmative scream still vibrated inside his skull. Adams raised his eyes from the foolscap, changed the ballpoint pen from right to left hand, then flexed the cramp from his right fingers. Lyle pushed himself slowly upright from the chair, walked to the wash basin, turned a tap and splashed cold water onto his face before wiping himself on the towel. Then he loosened the knot of his tie, as if that final effort had expended every last ounce of his breath and he needed unrestricted air-way to his lungs.

He glanced at his wrist-watch. It showed 5.10 a.m.

The thought flickered through his mind . . . it had been *some* night!

He walked back to the table, stood for a moment looking down at Barker, then said, 'It's done with. It's out. From here on it gets easier.'

Barker didn't seem to hear.

Lyle said, 'I know what I'm talking about, Barker. I've seen it happen too many times to have any doubt.'

Barker still didn't answer and Lyle walked to the chair, spun it to face the table and sat down.

He said, 'A statement, perhaps? It's the usual thing.'

'Why not?'

Barker did not raise his head when he answered the question with a counter-question. The two words were a whispered groan of defeat.

'I'm not pressing,' said Lyle gently. 'It's your decision. No pressure, for or against.'

'Will it help?' Barker slowly raised his head and stared across at Lyle. Wild-eyed. Pale as a man with a terminal disease. The faint stubble of an overnight beard showing on his chin and jowls. Hair awry. Even his moustache looking bedraggled and uncared for. 'Will it help?' he asked in a stronger voice. 'You? Me? Anybody? Will it help?'

'It gets the excuses down – the explanations – in black and white. It's read out in court. Your side of things.'

'Do I have a "side of things"?' asked Barker bitterly.

'The lies you've told, they needn't be repeated.'

'In court?'

'Anywhere. A statement, you start with a clean slate. The previous statements. We don't use them. There's no point. We don't rub it in.'

'You don't . . .' For a moment – for a split second – hysteria wasn't far from Barker's tone. Mad laughter seemed to tremble on his lips and his eyes widened with momentary mania. The near-hysteria switched to mild sarcasm. 'That's nice to know, inspector. That you don't rub it in. What am I facing? Three charges of murder. Three charges of child-rape. But never mind . . . you don't rub it in. That's very comforting.'

'We were talking about statements,' said Lyle flatly.

'Yes,' sighed Barker.

'Yes what?'

'Yes, I'll give you your precious statement, inspector. Yes . . . just tell me what you want me to say and I'll say it.'

Lyle said, 'Statement forms, please, sergeant.'

'Yes, sir.'

Adams stood up, placed the clip-board on the seat of the chair and left the all-purpose room.

It was cigarette-time again. Lyle provided them; the last two from his packet. He lit Barker's then his own.

He said, 'I'm – er – I'm sorry about Bell. Sergeant Bell. What he did. It wasn't necessary.'

'Obviously.'

'No, I mean . . .' For the first time Lyle seemed tongue-tied. He changed the subject. He said. 'Your wife's still here.'

'Oh, my God!'

'At least . . . ,' Lyle corrected himself, '. . . I think she is. She *was*. In one of the Interview Rooms.'

'What good is she doing?'

'Wives.' Lyle shrugged. 'Women generally. Who knows? They hide their feelings a lot.'

Barker smoked a quarter of an inch of cigarette, then said, 'She won't want to see me.'

'She might.'

'It's not important. I don't want to see her.' But the remark lacked complete conviction.

Lyle said, 'Cindy?'

'She'd no right . . .'

'She'd every right.' Lyle jerked his head to look into Barker's face. 'Cindy . . . Standish . . . Wallace . . . Roberts. It's a pattern. We needed that pattern. Cindy was a key.'

'Your key. Your pattern.'

'It's over. It's done with. Be grateful – try to be grateful – it stopped at Roberts.'

'My God!' Barker's lip curled slightly.

'I know.' Lyle nodded complete understanding. 'As you feel now. As you've felt since you strangled Roberts. "Never again. Never, *ever* again." But . . . you would have done.' For the first time genuine compassion cored Lyle's voice. 'You need treatment, Barker. Punishing? Certainly. But more than that – treatment. It's a sickness. It can be cured.'

'Should I put that in the statement?' asked Barker gently.

'If you think you should.' Lyle's tone was now gruff with embarrassment.

Adams returned with the statement forms; quarto-sized sheets of ruled paper. He placed them on the table in front of Barker and, with them, a cheap ballpoint pen borrowed from the Charge Office.

Lyle said, 'Your statement, Barker. Your own words. You've a choice. Write it yourself or dictate it to Sergeant Adams and he'll write it. But no paragraphs. No spaces into which words might be inserted.'

'I'll – er – I'll dictate it,' said Barker.

'Fine. But the first part you have to write yourself. What you might call a guarantee of authenticity. I'll tell you what to write.'

Barker picked up the ballpoint and positioned the sheets.

Lyle said, 'Ready? Good. Start off. I, George Barker, make this statement quite voluntarily . . .'

Barker wrote the words.

'. . . after having been told by Detective Inspector Lyle . . .'

Barker wrote the words.

'. . . that I am under no obligation to make this statement . . .'

Barker wrote the words.

'. . . and that I am not obliged to say anything unless I wish to do so . . .'

Barker wrote the words.

'. . . but that whatever I say including the contents of this statement . . .'

Barker wrote the words.

'. . . may be given in evidence.'

Barker wrote the words.

Lyle continued, 'I have elected to make this statement of my own accord . . .'

Barker wrote the words.

'. . . without threat, intimidation or promise of future reward.'

Barker wrote the words.

Lyle said, 'I have been asked whether I wish to write this statement myself . . .'

Barker wrote the words.

'. . . or whether I wish to dictate the statement and have it written for me.'

Barker wrote the words.

Lyle said, 'I have chosen to dictate the statement to Police Sergeant two-three-four-one Adams.'

Barker wrote the words.

'The full meaning of what you've just written,' said Lyle. 'Do you understand it or do you want any part of it explained to you?'

'I understand the Queen's English,' said Barker.

'Good. Now sign your name – on the next line – and add the time and date.' He glanced at his wrist-watch. 'The time is five-twenty-five.'

Barker signed his name, then added the time and date.

As Adams moved his chair to the table to take up a position next to Barker, Barker said, 'One thing, inspector. May I ask Sergeant Adams questions?'

'What sort of questions?'

'Locations? Minor details? Specific times? Things like that. For example Dane's Dyke, I've never heard the name before. And where I parked my car at Birkdale . . . I don't know the name of the street. Presumably you want a statement to be as accurate as possible.'

'He'll help you,' said Lyle carefully. 'Jog your memory, but only if you ask him. He won't put words into your mouth. But the statement's yours. Not his interpretation. As long as that's understood.'

'Understood.' Barker bobbed his head in acknowledgement.

Adams picked up the cheap ballpoint and slid the statement forms to within easy writing distance.

CHAPTER FORTY-TWO

Lyle mooched around the near-empty D.H.Q. building. Tired. Dry-throated with too much talking and too many cigarettes. Grubby, unwashed, unshaven and with that peculiar feeling of slovenliness which was unique to an all-night interview session. Odd; the night – the very darkness – seemed to deposit its own brand of dirt on a man's skin. Dirt which couldn't be removed without a good bath and a few hours' sleep.

Bobbying! Self-destruction for a pittance . . . nothing less. While sane men slept, you drove yourself to the edge in the name of communal vengeance. Three kids dead – three kids not yet in their teens – ravished, then strangled. And today – later on today – the news would go out. 'A man is helping the police with their enquiries'. And decent men would sigh and smile their satisfaction. The good old British bobby. He'd done it again. But those same decent men would, within hours, play blue hell if another 'British bobby' booked them for some road traffic offence.

And the needle would come from the other direction, too. Nothing surer. All the glory-hunters. The assistant chief constables and the detective chief superintendents and all the rest of the big-wigs. A lot of congratulations. A lot of back-slapping. But watch those eyes, friend; note that don't-try-it-on-again glint which goes with the smiles and the well-done phrases.

Bobbying! It took twenty-three years of solid graft – twenty-three years of missed meals and lost sleep – to become as cold-bloodedly cynical as Lyle. It wasn't easy. Nor was it cheap; the price included friends and sometimes wives and families. But in return you got something unique. Not particularly nice, but unique. It was known as 'a police mind'. A gift. An expertise. The ability to take a fellow-man and peel the skins away from him, like peeling an onion. To feel no pain. To see no pain. To have no pity. To know that the great, boozed-up, Bingo-playing, pop-oriented, football-crazy, television-addicted British public still took it for granted that their policemen were 'wonderful'.

That three kids had met a particularly horrific death, but that their killer would kill no more.

Swings and roundabouts. One made you dizzy, the other made you sick. Make your choice, Lyle, and give thanks you've only two more years to go. But never did a pension come more costly.

He was almost surprised to find himself in the Interview Room. It had not been a conscious journey. He hadn't meant to wander his way back to the room where Barker's wife still waited. He'd just . . . arrived there.

He closed the door, flopped onto the vacant chair, leaned back, with his head resting against the wall and sprawled there, legs wide and eyes staring at the ceiling. He remained like that for a few moments, then moved his head, saw the opened packet of cigarettes on the table and, without even asking, helped himself.

She watched him in silence. Three minutes (give a second, take a second) eased themselves into contemporary history.

Then she said, 'He's confessed.'

It was a statement, not a question.

Lyle nodded.

She said, 'It's taken longer than I expected.'

'He's a lot to lose.'

'What . . . exactly?'

'His life.' Lyle looked directly at her for the first time.

'He'll get life. There'll be a recommendation attached. He'll be lucky if it's less than twenty-five years.'

'He'll be an old man.'

'Lady, he won't live it out.' Lyle's tone was harsh and pitiless. 'He'll be no ordinary prisoner. The lags will make his life hell. Given the chance they'll cripple him. Given a free hand they'll kill him. The authorities know that . . . that men who are, themselves, scum become maudlin and sentimental when it comes to children. The authorities will protect him the only way they know how. Solitary confinement. As near as makes no difference. I've seen men who've suffered it . . . for a lot less than twenty-five years. To them the abolition of hanging was a retrograde step.'

'Oh, my God!'

'It's what you wanted, madam.' There was a soft but furious disgust in Lyle's voice. 'It's what *I* wanted. This so-called civilised community demands it. We must not, now, cry in our beer.'

'We mustn't forget . . . We mustn't forget . . .'

She stumbled over the words and couldn't go on. She stared at Lyle and her eyes pleaded for sympathy. For some relief upon which she might hang the rest of her life.

'We mustn't forget the children.' Lyle completed the sentence for her. He drew hard on the cigarette, then continued, 'No, indeed, we must not forget the children. Cindy, for example.'

'Cindy?'

Lyle hauled himself into a more upright position. He knew she was pleading for comfort, but instead he gave her a cold, brutal accusation.

He said, 'Your husband. Men like him. They're in a minority . . . but it's not an insignificant minority. They're twisted . . . all right, they're twisted. But they hide it. And they're *helped* to hide it. Their families. Their wives. Their brothers, sisters . . . everybody. This damned "respectability". It's like having an alcoholic in the family. Nobody else must know. It's a disgrace. A skeleton in the cupboard . . . so let's close the door and keep it locked.

'So – eventually – they kill. Their continued "respectability" demands it. Who the devil wants "respectability" at that price?' He cocked an eyebrow at her, then answered his own question. '*You* do. You and thousands like you. Cindy was the tip of the iceberg. You knew it, but you chose to ignore it. You and your brother and your sister-in-law. For Cindy's sake . . . three children had to die "for Cindy's sake".

'He needs treatment. He needed treatment five years ago. You knew it, you're not a fool, but you chose to ignore it. You chose to punish him instead. How did you put it? "Played properly a woman can make her husband feel unclean". You played it well, madam. You played the wrong game – you're the dominant partner, you could have forced him to seek treatment, seek help – but you played the wrong game . . . and you played it very skilfully.'

Lyle pushed himself to his feet. He screwed out the cigarette in the base of the tobacco tin.

As he opened the door to leave the Interview Room he said, 'For the record, madam. I'm undecided. I don't know who I despise most . . . you, me, or your husband.'

CHAPTER FORTY-THREE

By twenty minutes after six o'clock the night-shift men had gone home to their beds. The 'early-turn' crew – the six-to-two officers – were already on the streets in their squad cars, at their desks and at the switchboard. The uniformed chief inspector had left. Adams's relief had taken over in the Charge Office. The day was gradually winding itself up into its regular, steady tempo.

The teleprinter clacked and spewed out its message.

Lyle, more asleep than awake, leaned against the wall of the Charge Office warming his rump on one of the radiators. The bitterness and self-disgust was still with him. It still gnawed at his mind like a nibbling rodent. Odd . . . some cases affected him that way. Cases where the basic fault lay in weakness. Where the trigger for the crime – any crime – was lack of understanding. In a back-to-front sort of way he enjoyed the chase – the pitting of wits – against the accused, but the kill sickened him. When the man cracked, that was when the self-hate took over. It was why, whenever possible, he landed another officer with the job of statement-taking. Somebody like Adams; somebody who didn't seem to mind recording the outpourings of a warped personality; the piffling excuses, which were never the real excuses; the pleading and the snivelling, the cries for help and the empty phrases, all of which would end up as eye-catching quotes in some daily scandal-rag.

'And the greatest of these is charity' . . . Lyle's wandering mind touched a long-forgotten thread of memory. He was not a religious man, but at that moment the words seemed to encapsulate just about everything wrong with the system of which he was a part.

The woman police constable at the teleprinter ripped the latest message from the machine. She hesitated a moment then, having made a decision, she walked across the Charge Office to Lyle.

She handed the typed message to Lyle and said, 'I think you should see this, sir.'

Lyle's eyes widened, then he blinked them to rid them of the half-sleep. He read the teleprinter message, stone-faced except for a slight tightening of the jaw-line.

He glanced at the switchboard and said, 'Get me an outside line, please. I'll take it from the super's office.'

CHAPTER FORTY-FOUR

Adams was squaring up the statement forms as Lyle entered the all-purpose room. Barker was still sitting at the table. He had a strange dead expression on his face.

Adams said, 'Just in time, sir. Signed, sealed and delivered.'

'A full statement?'

'Yes, sir.'

'All three murders?'

'Yes, sir.'

'How much help from you, sergeant?'

'The usual.' Adams made a vague gesture with his right hand. 'The exact times. Locations. Odd bits and pieces he'd forgotten ... that's all.'

Lyle closed the door very gently. The impression was that he tip-toed to the table, then stood looking down at Barker.

'Why?' he asked and his voice was soft, but harsh.

Barker looked up and said, 'The excuses – the explanations – they're all in the statement, inspector. As you said ...'

'No. I don't mean that. I mean *why*?'

Barker frowned puzzlement, then said, 'I don't understand. It's what you ...'

'This.' Lyle moved the teleprinter message which he still held. 'From the Birmingham police. It came in a few minutes ago. I've double-checked it. Six o'clock last night. A nine-year-old girl was attacked. She was being dragged into a wood of some sort. A coppice. Two men – farm-workers – heard her screams. They grabbed the man. Called the police. The Birmingham C.I.D. interviewed him. Most of the night. He knows things about the

Standish killing, the Wallace killing, the Roberts killing
... things only the murderer can know. A long-distance
lorry driver. Remember the Standish kid? It fits. It fits
perfectly. He's been charged. He's up in front of a magis-
trate later this morning. Now, why?' He tapped the tiny
pile of statement forms with the tip of a forefinger. 'In
God's name, why *this*?'

Adams breathed, 'For Christ's sake!'

Barker looked at Adams, then back at Lyle. His mouth
opened and closed, but no words came. Sweat marbled
his forehead, then ran in tiny rivulets down his ashen
face. For a moment it looked as if he might pass out.

Lyle deliberately controlled himself. He lowered himself
onto the chair vacated by Adams and, in a steady, gentle,
pleading voice, he said, 'Mr Barker. Will you *please* tell
me why?'

'It's – it's – it's . . .' Barker shook his head as if to clear
his mind of dust and cobwebs. He ran the palm and
fingers of one hand across his face to wipe away the sweat.
Then he took two deep, lung-expanding breaths and, in a
still tremulous voice, said, 'It's – it's hard to explain.'

'Try,' pleaded Lyle.

'It could have been.' Barker moved his head fractionally and stared, unseeing, at a point mid-way down the
surface of the table. His voice took on a monotonic, sing-
song quality; part-moan, part-berceuse; soft and over-
flowing with long-accepted defeat. It was the voice a
spectre might use, when intoning the sins for which it
remains restless. 'It – it could have been me. You were so
sure. So very sure. Edwina – my wife . . . she's *still* sure.
She won't believe. Whoever else . . . she'll never believe it
was him. Me. She'll always believe it was me.

'That's why. I – I couldn't prove it wasn't. Everybody
said it was. I told lies. Silly. I should have told the truth.
From the first, I should have told the truth. But I told

lies. Silly lies. But – but I was ashamed. So ashamed. The – the women. The prostitutes. Other – other men go with prostitutes . . . I suppose they do. But Edwina . . . What would she have . . . ? And – and I did touch Gwendolen. The – the blood. And she was so – so cold. So – so . . . I was frightened. The other two . . . then Gwendolen. It *had* to be me. Who else? Who in the world would believe it *wasn't* me? After – after Cindy? Who would ever believe?

'And . . . I was tired. So tired. The police. Questioned by the police after each murder. Doing their job . . . they were only doing their job. They had to see me. But . . . for six months! It's been me for six months. *Me*. Edwina. The police. And tonight, you. I was tired of making the denial. The same denial. And nobody ever really believing me. Even when I told the truth. You *still* didn't believe me.

'So . . . let it be me. That's all. It could have been me, so *let* it be me. It didn't matter anymore. It still doesn't matter. Not really. Let it be me. I'm past caring.' He raised his head, focused lustreless eyes on Lyle's face, and ended, 'That's why, inspector. You understand . . . surely?'

Lyle nodded. Slowly, but without real conviction.

He lifted the statement forms from the table, held them towards Adams and said, 'Tear them up, sergeant. And the notes.'

'Yes, sir.'

'And – er . . .' Lyle pushed himself to his feet. Suddenly he looked old beyond his years. He murmured, 'The usual forms and formalities. He's been arrested. Bail. To this police station in – say – fourteen days. Then arrange for the bail to be cancelled. The usual "unarrest" rigmarole. You know the pattern.'

'Yes, sir.'

'I'll – er – I'll have a word with his wife. Tell her what's happened.'

CHAPTER FORTY-FIVE

As he reached the Interview Room Lyle heard the uniformed constable calling his name. He waited.

The constable was breathless and a little scared.

He stammered, 'Sir . . . Mrs Barker. Outside. Just now. I was just coming to find you. To tell you. She – she stepped off the pavement . . . straight in front of a bus. Deliberately. Dozens of witnesses. The driver hadn't a chance. She's – she's . . .'

'Dead?'

The word fell like a boulder into a black pond.

The constable nodded.

CHAPTER FORTY-SIX

The superintendent looked puzzled.

He'd driven to the D.H.Q. building along his usual route, along the lesser-used side roads in order to avoid the traffic and into the car park at the rear via the back gates. He'd missed the mêlée of the fatal accident at the front of the building.

He walked into the Charge Office and questioned the early-shift office-duty sergeant.

He said, 'What the hell? Has something happened? I've just passed Inspector Lyle in the car park. He looked – I dunno . . . he looked like a damn corpse. And, for God's sake, he was *crying*!'

3 1220 00150 4049
PORTLAND PUBLIC LIBRARY

fiction WAINWRI, JOHN
Wainwright, John William,
1921-
Brainwash

PORTLAND PUBLIC LIBRARY
5 MONUMENT SQUARE
PORTLAND, ME 04101